Lovedemic

Poetry and problems

Papikins

Cyrus Ahmadnia

Papikins

Lovedemic

Copyright © 2021 by Cyrus Ahmadnia (Papikins)

This book is a creative work of fiction, and should be treated as such.

ISBN 978-1-9168832-4-6 (Paperback)

ISBN 978-1-9168832-5-3 (eBook)

Published by Papikins Publishing

www.papikins.com

Papikins

Lovedemic

For those who seek solace in the sun and the moon, and in the stars and the clouds. This is for the quiet one who awaits for affection and distraction.

This is for the broken.

Papikins

Table of contents

Papikins

Lovedemic

Papikins

Papikins

Lovedemic

I've lost all concept of time. I blink and everything is gone, from the memories I held to the moments I once felt. I tried to ease the pain with distractions when I could, but now I'm here alone, wondering what the fuck to do. Am I destined to be stuck inside of solitude? The pandemic has taken over, and I've gone deeper down into the blue. The days are getting colder, as winter is creeping back into my view. It's a beautiful time of year, yet it hurts me to be here. I wanted to be remembered, but I'm forgetting who I am. It's the loneliness that's killing me, but I've always felt alone, even when being close to others, because they only disappear. The problem has always been that I never want to smile, and when I do, it's painted on my lips. I look into the mirror and all I see are fragments of what was and who I never got to be. I'm a poet. I'm a wanderer. I'm the death of love and the start of something sinister.

I've always wanted to connect to people. I've wanted them to see me the way I never had the chance to see myself. I hide my imperfections, and it only leaves a scar that never seems to heal. We're full of scars and sadness. It's the ground we lay our feet on, isn't it? We can never perceive it as being solid, so we stumble but never break our fall. We search for someone out there who can show us more than what we know, and when we find them, we dream about tomorrow. We let each other in and suddenly the light shines down on to the darkness. We find ourselves alone together, and as

1

Lovedemic

the worries slip away, we want to take romance to the grave. I want that again, but everything seems to end. All the times I said 'I love you' are drowned out by the silence. I'm stuck reliving what I had before, and I'm pulling at my strings to hold myself together. I thought I could trust in someone else, but now my heart's been shattered. It's love. It weakens us completely, yet we're addicted to the taste of what could be. I'm hopeless and distraught. I always seem to chase romantic dreams, but when I'm close enough to touch what I desire, I get burnt as if I'm playing with nothing more than fire.

The world has numbed me to the core. I've lost all touch of who I was before. I used to be alive but now I'm just too tired. It takes a toll when you've been sheltered, and it's a part of why I feel so helpless. I'm always looking for release, and when I can't express the reasons why I'm like this, I fall into distress. I keep thinking, and I keep thinking, but where do I go from there? The thoughts are all the same, and the ones which bring me joy only seem to float away. I truly wanted to find myself in love, but an overthinker only ruins what they have. It isn't our intention, but we can never be as close as what we thought of. We can somehow feel corruption, and what we have suddenly turns into a burden. I connected all the pieces of betrayal and found that the love I had to give wasn't worth my time at all.

Love is just like poison. It's fatal when it sets. I never knew how hard it would be to find myself again. I was lost and alone, just like I am right now. The unimaginable truth is that people eventually

Papikins

drift too far, and what they had before is dead and gone. It's romance, isn't it? We learn to live together but are too stubborn to say goodbye. It's as if we create distance between us by not understanding that we're not meant to be, and believe me, I know it hurts to see it fade before your eyes, but endless love is just another lie. I'm sorry if you disagree, and I'm sorry if you're stuck believing you can change direction. There's no going back to what once was. It's a sad truth that many will deny. Believe me, I've been there one too many times. I had to look away from truth to keep my jaded smile. I didn't want to be alone, yet I still was. It's one thing to be alone by yourself, but to be alone when you're next to someone else is what prevents us from going further. We don't realise how little time we have, and when we stay in a place where neither of us should remain, we resent what we've become.

The loneliness is all I seem to know, as I sit in the comfort of my home. I sometimes wander towards these thoughts of love and wonder why the promises were never kept. I used to wish I could have been enough to make you stay, but never realised I was holding on to what we had. You were my escape when I felt like my walls were closing in. You were the breath behind my lungs, and the bitter taste between my tongue. We can never forget the one we loved, even if we want to. We're pulled towards the past because we were once attached. It's attachment, isn't it? We connect so seamlessly, yet in the end, we wonder if our stories were just pretence. I've always been afraid of opening my heart to others. I'm not sure if they'll love me in my entirety, or if they'll harm my peace.

Papikins

Lovedemic

I wanted to find myself in loneliness without running from the emptiness. We run from life so easily, but when we're trapped, we want to regain everything we had.

We never realise how precious emotions are, because we're left dissatisfied by problems that arise. The pandemic made many feel as though they've died, but struggle is a part of life, and I'll be damned if I let anything steal my shine. We neglect the truth at times. It's hard to see when you've been living in a lie. There have been times where I've felt alone, and I thought the end was getting closer, but I continued to survive. It's what we don't seem to realise. We let the hurt last a lifetime, but when our lives go on, we age away from what we were. It's a bitter truth to a bitter life. We barely live within the present, and when our time comes for realisation, it's too late to fix mistakes that we've been making. The truth is, they can never be fixed. They can only be accepted.

I've had a history of regret, and it pained me to lose my smile. I had this fear of being perfect because I was scared I couldn't reach it, and I was right. We're made from heartbreak and mistakes. We look back too much to find escape, because we're still living in the past. There's nothing perfect about what we had. It's the reason why it haunts us. It's the reason why the empty spaces remain vacant. We have no intention to grow from who we were, so we try to numb the ache. I didn't want to run. I knew there was something I could change. I just needed some time to think, and luckily, we were somehow locked away. Welcome to the Lovedemic. I sincerely hope you enjoy your visit.

Papikins

Poetry

What is poetry? It's whatever I want you to believe. I disregard conformity, as I create beauty without dishonesty. I want to be your hurt and happiness, even if after all of this, you forget that I exist.

Problems

Papikins

We lose ourselves in moments. Some are beautiful while others only hurtful. We want to run from what we know and fade into the scenery, but our problems aren't resolved. It isn't our intention to disconnect entirely, but sometimes, we twist and turn without direction. We live to be alive, but when there is no life, we only live to die.

Lovedemic

Alpha

I'm atrociously imperfect.

Papikins

Mirror

There are places where my mind will wander. They remind me of the person that I lost and the sadness that came after. I remember you. I remember what it felt to be connected and ultimately fade into the distance. The problem is, I don't see you anymore when looking back into the mirror—I'm someone else entirely.

The mask

I'm sorry. It's hard to be myself when everyone expects me to be perfect. I've tried to show another side of me that no one ever wants to know. It's my truth. It's the part of me that exists only when I'm alone. I have a thousand stories but they only lead to hell, and the saddest truth is, they're too exhausting for me to tell. It's easier to wear a mask than it is to be exposed. I'm afraid of infecting everyone around me with the fears I hold inside. It feels as though a part of me has died. I chased the world repeatedly, but as I came close enough to match its flight, it disappeared before my eyes. I never knew how small I was until staring at the sky. It was endless, and there was nowhere it could hide. It reminded me of all the times I've tried yet fell short on being happy in my life. I sometimes wish I could go back. I want to change myself and what I had, but then I'd only be feeding the addiction I have towards the past.

I've never been able to see myself like others do. Maybe it's self-perception, or what I lack in clarity. I wonder what life is, and where I even fit. I've pushed myself to change, but I'm pulled apart by sadness. It's depressing to even think where I'll be when I reach the end. I write these words to give me strength, yet as the letters are stained in ink, I still feel as though I'm weak. I need to find release. I need to take the weight off of my shoulders so I can catch my breath. I barely trust myself at times. It's the loneliness that ruins me. I give, and I give, but when everything is taken, I'm left with

Papikins

nothing in return. I used to be there for anyone who asked, because I didn't want them to be the way I am. I deserve someone to save me, but I guess it isn't in God's plan.

I'm tired of expectations that I can never reach. I'm treated like an outcast when I'm far away in dreams. No one understands me, or maybe it's how it seems. I feel indifferent when surrounded, like I shouldn't share a moment with the ones around me. I try to trust in others, yet all I find are reasons to drift further from where I'm standing. I've been holding on to friends who wouldn't care if I was there. I always seem to fall within distractions. I attach myself to people until I tear apart my walls and let them in to ruin me. I'm a fucking a tragedy. I want them to notice how much I'm trying, but I only don a mask. It isn't me entirely, but it's all I have to give. It hurts, you know? We try to be a perfect person, yet no one ever stays. Nothing ever seems consistent. We want someone to find us in the cold, but we're only left deserted.

The worst part about me has always been my history. I've wanted to erase the tears I've shed, but they're still running through my head. I feel neglected and unwanted, but maybe that's the narrative I've set. I push away when I'm craving to be heard. I just want to feel a little more than hurt. It's all I ask for when I'm drowning in these thoughts. I wore my smile so beautifully, but as the years went on, it was painted with regret. I forced myself to feel, but all I felt were unsung melodies and chills. I have moments I wish I could have had, but they never went to plan. I was too far gone, too soon. I remember what it meant to love, but if I couldn't love

Papikins

myself, was I meant to give my heart away for pleasure or for pain? It's hard, you know? I've always worn a mask. I've hidden secrets to extend my state of happiness. It's how I cope with stress. It's how I keep the strings tied around my face. I don't want anyone to see me beyond my masquerade.

It's simplicity that carries so much beauty, and I've simply kept my secrets just to be. It's all I can ask for when I'm running from the cold. I've had my share of disappointment and I've tried to bear it all, but when my heart is bleeding blue, I only lack control. I try to fight away the ice, but it projects my history into my shallow eyes. I've told a thousand tales, but the saddest ones are when I'm in disguise. I don't know who I am, yet I try to dabble in connection, but in the end, reality shines through, and I have to say goodbye to what was never true. It's the mask. It's my way of not being held accountable for all the wrong I do. I use it as an excuse. I use it to make sense of why I feel so blue. I disconnect so easily. I stick within the shadows until it's time to finally be seen. I want to burn the mask to smithereens, but there's a problem—the mask has always had a name, but I never had a chance to greet it without crying. The truth is, there was no mask to see, it was just another side of me.

Papikins

Ship

I'm holding on to all the memories of us, from when we were in love to when you lost my trust. It isn't easy living with deceit. You tore apart my walls and belittled my beliefs. I romanticized your eyes, and fell deep within your aching smile. I knew that I would falter if I ever let you in, but the risk was worth the reward of finding love again. I witnessed beauty deep within you, and it hurts to say that you are now an issue. We sailed the seas together, learning what it meant to live in trying times. Through all of our endeavours, you were everything I hoped for, and maybe just a little more. It's sad to say that our ship never made it to the shore.

A tale of sadness

She lived for friends and family, but no one trusted her completely. They brought up past mistakes which she never should have made. She put herself in situations which only harmed her health, but she never realised that she's the one to blame. I could tell you she was perfect, but I'd only be a liar. We write stories based on what we see, and if I only gave her praise, it wouldn't be as hurtful as I intended it to be. She would walk across the street while tapping pavement lines against her feet. She was unusual. She loved to feel as if she's free, but with freedom comes a tale which no one could ever see. The problem is, she trusted too much with her fragile heart. She wanted sunsets and butterflies to appear before her tired eyes, but what she found was a monster in disguise. It's a story some may know too well, because love sometimes leads to hell. She wanted to be loved more than the Earth itself, but never realised, there were those who cared for themselves more than saving lives.

She was screaming out for love, because she was conditioned to believe it would give her strength when she was lost. It was all that crossed her mind. She wanted to fall into another's arms and ink her chapters in a perfect shade of black. She craved to have affection, because she only ever felt like she's an option. The ones who left only tore her flaws apart until her confidence was taken. She was reminded of the reasons why she barely ever loved. She was only used for lust. They never saw her as forever, as she was constantly replaced. She desperately wanted to find her place, but after every ending, she'd wipe the tears away from her sculpted face. She was tired of repeating her mistakes, yet her past seemed to always be replayed. When you look beyond a smile, you can view a universe which is only shared by one. She hid her insecurities, because they only made her want to run.

She would sit with friends and wonder why she could barely stand at all. She was frozen still because she had nowhere else to go. It's the saddest place which she could be in. She never fit as much as she had wanted. The echoes of their voices only made her feel alone. She would try to cover up her stillness by twiddling her thumbs, as she sat there feeling numb. She was wild at heart, but reserved when surrounded by those who showed no trust. The truth is, she had to wear a mask to be comfortable with decisions that were never made to last. She would suddenly find the urge to be more active, and as her darkness was released, her actions were impulsive. She wanted to be like everyone around her, but the more she broke out of her shell, the more she'd lose herself.

There are always a thousand faces when it comes to people. One may be quiet while another more persistent. We shift in and out of character based on how we feel. She was no stranger to emotions. She knew them well enough to make her sleepless. She would lay awake in bed, wondering why she felt confusion in her head. There were thoughts of what she wanted and pictures of what she had. They intertwined in all their beauty, but suddenly they were burnt into the ground. Her thoughts were tragic, yet they somehow gave her peace. It was the tears. They were formed to give release. She cried on many nights, but what hurt the most was that she wanted someone laying by her side. She wanted to be held. It's how she thought love could save her soul, but little did she know, the future is never set in stone.

The world is beautiful. We wander into realms of possibility, as we aim to find connection. She wanted her story to stay consistent, but she prayed that she could find solace inside another person. The truth is, she never truly loved herself as much as she should have. She would throw around her worth and wish it would be enough to make love stay. She was attached to the idea of giving herself away. She was so tired. She wanted to believe she had more to give than a body made to fade. She was so gifted. I'm surprised no one ever knew. They never wanted to see her scars, or see the memories which were carved into her heart. No one could see behind her broken smile, that is until she finally met me. How do these stories go? We always wonder what the future holds. We're curious to see what happens in the cold. I just want to give you a glimpse before I go.

I had every intention to understand why she felt so distant. I wanted to close the space between us, but all I ever did was hurt her in the process. I told you, I don't want to be a liar. Every letter that I write is a part of something I remember, and I remember her more than every tomorrow that came after. I've never felt enough, and I guess we shared each other's sadness. It's dangerous, isn't it? We connect to those who share our pain, but because we've lived a life

15

Papikins

of misery, we barely get a chance to write our story. I saw through everything she ever did, and I was amazed beyond description. She was a newly found addiction as I spiralled in and out of her seduction. We told each other secrets which were never shared with those around us. I finally felt weightless when I was lost in her embrace. The problem is, we repeatedly pushed away. We would hardly speak for days and it would only cause a strain. We were bleeding black and blue. It isn't any wonder why we felt so bruised.

I found her eyes enchanting. They were full of depth and filled with life and death. They spoke a thousand words when all we had was silence. The first time we ever kissed, I could feel her past against my lips. She had a fear of being open, and as she backed away, I knew she was scared to love again. It's the little things she did which made me wonder where we stand. She gave me honesty but in return, I gave her a shoulder she could cry on. I'm the worst kind of person. I attach only for affection. I want to feel close to being human, so I give until every part of me is taken. There are times where she'd detach and I felt like I'm the reason. It's how we blame ourselves when thinking. I never meant to part the space between us, but sometimes, we see ourselves a little different. I wanted to be the saviour she was begging me to be, but little did I know, the only one who needed to be saved was me.

Attachment sometimes brings you pain. She was tired of how we were, as we'd argue out of spite. We were fixing mistakes every single day, but nothing could erase what we would say. We held anger in our hearts, and the apologies didn't seem enough. We both

16

had issues with our trust. It happens when you drift too far apart. We'd distract ourselves with other people, because we didn't want to stare at the death of something beautiful. We once ruled the world together. She let me in when all she felt was shattered, and in return, I only gave her silence. When we were together, everywhere was home, just as long as we had each other close. But after all the bickering, I couldn't keep pretending. I sometimes sabotage myself, and I end up more alone. We changed beyond what we both knew. We never should have overstayed our welcome, but it's what lovers seem to do.

She fell backwards into problems she wanted to avoid, and when we were together, all she felt was noise. The calmness we once had somehow disappeared, and all that was left were the memories we shared. She was back to wearing her disguise, and I knew we were running out of time. I felt it too. I was scared of conversations and giving her attention. We weren't the same as what we used to be. She'd attach herself to people who were the opposite of me. It was what she wanted, and deep down, I just wanted us to fade. We were too stubborn to say goodbye, so all we did was stay. We were both a part of why we lost our spark. We were too comfortable with what we had, and suddenly, we felt nothing, even when holding hands.

There's no escaping from the truth. We were trying to run when we were out of fuel. I was done. I was tired of keeping her in place. I wanted to be more selfish. I forgot about myself, as I tried so hard to give her strength. I wanted to save her more than anything, but that was a problem in itself. She reminded me of my reflection. It was the only reason why I didn't mind the distance. We were both in love with the idea of connection, but our minds began to weaken. We felt too far away from reach and never had a chance to chase the dream. I couldn't help but fill myself with anger, and every word would suddenly get louder. I'd snap instantly. I couldn't stop these thoughts of why our love could never be enough. I hated us. I hated me, and I hater her, yet still I tried my best to stay. It's stupidity, isn't it? Real love is unlike fairy tales. We slip and we slide. We dip and we lie. I knew it was time to stop hurting for the both of us, but at that point, there was nothing left but loss.

The truth is, I create worlds inside my head and hope to find somewhere I'll be safe. We were what we needed, but it was never close to fate. It's attraction, isn't it? I saw promise in what was there, but I barely saw the future. She was addictive yet destructive, or maybe that was me. I can never separate the two at times, because both of us were to blame for what we had and all our crimes. We were feeding into addiction rather than connecting for completion. You never quite realise how hurtful love can be until reality becomes a memory. We wanted to be happy, but we were tired of standing in each other's shadows. I had to find the strength to leave. It was written on every single star. It was destiny. I slipped away in silence, as she surrounded herself with who she had before. We were just another heartfelt tragedy, and I just hope she remembers me. Maybe one day our paths will cross again, but for now, our tale of sadness remains without an end.

Papikins

Beautiful distraction

You were a beautiful distraction. I had been longing to find a sense of safety, and you sheltered me from the fear of being lonely. You were the fire beneath my feet as I tried so hard to run. You were the ache inside my heart and the reason why I felt so numb. You gave me life within my breath, and I wish you all the best.

Yours sincerely,

The one you left.

A tale of sorrow

He lost himself in thoughts, as he pushed to love again. He had always been so hopeless, and romance was his weakness. He felt the urge to fill the empty space, but never truly felt anything could take its place. Love was all he ever thought about, and he wanted to believe he could find it when he lacked the will to love himself. It never occurred to him how hard he'd fall if he continued to lose control. He would stare out into fields and wonder why the sun was close but far away. He wanted to be connected to strangers he met along the way, but sadly, no one felt the same. They would see his flaws and how his personality was chained. He could never be himself, not even when alone. He was fighting with demons of the past and it was all he ever knew. There was a silence in the air, yet the sound of chaos was all that he could hear. It was always the silence which left him in despair. It was never as clear as he had hoped, and all it ever did was make him choke.

He had been afraid to bare his soul, and he'd cover up his eyes so his humanity would rarely show. It was the darkness. It kept him tied down to a leash, and he couldn't seem to breathe. He wanted to start his life somewhere outside of all the blue, but the cold would pull him back as if he was being dragged by a thousand hands. There was nowhere he felt safe, not even in his home. It was the thoughts. They always kept their hold. He was drowning in his mistakes, and he never learnt with age. He was full of promise, but

Papikins

he rarely ever noticed. He put himself down whenever he fell apart in sadness. It was never easy being left with intrusive thoughts of why he could never feel enough. They were haunting. He would lay awake at night, contemplating on all the times he's cried, but he fell deeper into what he had in life. He was never satisfied, not even when he felt alive.

The world had always been so closed. He would repeat his days and live within the shadows. He could never show himself the way he wanted, because he was scared he'd never finish what he started. He would carry himself with words, but his actions were never as constant as he stated. He was never present. He couldn't be. He was unusual. He would try to find himself in others, but they only added to his troubles. The truth is, he would stay stuck inside his bubble, and as the nights continued, he'd detach himself from people. His friends were unforgiving. They never understood that he was grieving. He had lost himself completely, yet had no chance of building back the walls that were torn apart by septic memories. He was pleasing everyone around him, even when he found it hard to breathe. It was another distraction to keep him far away from breaking. He had to surround himself with ghosts to stop himself from shaking.

It was always the term ghosts which hit the hardest. The people he once knew would disappear behind the madness. They'd never be consistent, not even when he was begging to be saved. There was a constant stream of friendship, yet none would ever stay. He was cruising through without a cause, and there was no substance to feed his troubled soul. He was spiralling out of control. His needs were incapable of being filled. He pushed for change yet never felt he'd reach perfection. He would walk away from problems, but never knew they'd only return to haunt him. He couldn't face the truth. He placed his trust in strangers, but in the end, they gave him reasons to be cautious. There was an anger building deep inside him. He wanted to burn his pages, but there was nothing he could do to erase the time he wasted. The saddest part of every story is when you get to see behind another's eyes. It gives you a sense of calmness, but when there's only chaos, you're left speechless.

He was a mess. He was searching for someone to fit within his universe, but no one brought out the side of him which only existed within loneliness. He had little hope to find his meaning, until he finally met me. I was in love with romantic dreams, and when I felt his presence, the world had stopped within its tracks. I was never one to be reliable, but he gave me comfort. He gave me reasons to believe I could be wanted. It's all I ever hoped for, and I couldn't ask for more. We spent many nights together, expressing how we've felt in our endeavours. His smirk would make me melt. It was devious yet calming. I never knew where life would take us, or what was exactly coming. We found ourselves too close, too soon. We were just glad to experience more than our shortcomings.

I wanted to believe that love had found me, but sometimes, I'm lost between the spaces of what is and what could be. I was unsure of how to fight the urge of falling. I thought I was undeserving, but in his arms, I knew he was my one true calling. We were connected

22

beyond what I could feel. I knew he felt it too, but the way my life had been, it seemed to be unreal. I was clutching on to moments, not knowing where I am. I lost myself in love, yet I had no reasons to belong. It's how the world had been. It's how I think at times. I'm constantly under pressure of trying to be perfect, but what I couldn't see was that destruction seems to follow me. I remember his eyes. They were dark and beautiful, yet hidden behind his pupils were a lifetime of disguises. I could never really tell who he was when we were sitting close together. There were signs of secrets which never made it to the surface. I was scared. I knew my heart was fragile, and I kept expecting to be left behind like I have before.

We would walk along the crowded streets, but it was only ever just the two of us. He would slide his fingers into mine, and our hands would perfectly align. The warmth of his skin was all I ever needed to feel safe within our cold embrace. He taught me many things about myself which I never knew existed. He taught me I could be strong enough to fall in love. He was kind and he was sweet, but all that I could think about was why he was standing here with me. I've never felt enough. I throw myself into situations to feel a sense of purpose, and when I met him, I was somehow at my lowest. I was aching to be loved, because all I've ever felt had been neglected. The truth is, stories are all we ever have when we're left with nothing, and this is the story that I'm sharing.

There's a certain kind of loss attached to love. I never knew exactly what it was until our disconnect. I would sometimes need to catch my breath, and suddenly, days would pass and I couldn't find

Papikins

the courage to let him in again. I created space between us to find peace when I was scared. It put a strain on what we had, but we'd slowly come together like nothing ever happened. I didn't realise I was wrong. There are many unwritten rules to connection, and distance is what eventually disconnects us. The more we pushed away, the more apparent it became. We were holding on to a dying love, and it was hard to come to terms with. We fought and we fought, but nothing could be solved. We were only hurting one another. I never wanted to be put in a position where I'd feel less than what I had before, but when it comes to romance, it hurts to be alone.

We somehow fell too hard. I remember the sound of his voice, but now it only echoes through my head. We fed each other lies to keep our love alive. I wanted to believe we'd last forever, but we couldn't, even if we tried. Our minds were somewhere else, and we never had the chance to give each other more than what we have. I wanted him to be mine. I truly did. We were holding on to time, and we knew the end would one day come. He changed so easily. It was as if the person I once knew had somehow been erased. What we felt before had slowly waned. The situations had piled up, and we had to give each other space so we could deal with what we lost. We had nowhere left to hide, but a thousand places we could run. It's how love is. You feel like you've met the one until you hate what you've become.

We were all I ever dreamed about, but as we built our doubts, there wasn't enough love to go around. The times we spent together became a distant blur. I couldn't trust him when he barely trusted me. I hoped it would be different, but all these stories feel the same. They make me feel as though I'm dying. There was nothing I could do to save us. I had to let go of the most beautiful part of life. I had to let go of us. We were both to blame for what was going on, but I couldn't stand the disrespect. All I ever wanted was someone to help me love myself, but he made me feel like I was living to be somebody else. It was the arguments that pushed us to the edge. His temper would get the best of him, and to be honest, mine would do the same. We were close yet far apart, and that's what made it worse. We couldn't stand the sight of what we're losing. It was out of our control. We thought we were made for more, but didn't realise our bond was only tearing.

We'd suddenly show aggression, and the shouting wouldn't stop. I had to get away from what we were. I wasn't ready to leave behind the love we shared, but for the betterment of both of us, I had to go back to being friends. The sad truth is, I haven't seen him ever since. I wanted to, but as I fell into old habits, he was gone without a word. It's what he does when he's afraid. He could never handle honesty, and honestly, it's the part of him that ruined me. We barely stayed true to all our oaths. I hope we meet again tomorrow, but our tale of sorrow remains stagnant in the cold. I still wonder if he's out there, and if he remembers me at all, but I guess he sees me as just another ghost.

Papikins

Beta

If we were meant to be, why does it feel so wrong? You have somebody else, yet I still chase you with my love.

Papikins

Gamma

We place our trust in wolves, and in the end, our friends turn into ghosts.

Papikins

Delta

There's a light at the end of every tunnel, but no one ever tells you how to fight away the darkness. It isn't any wonder why we feel alone. We're fending off the demons with little help at all.

Papikins

Imperfect

The world is going crazy. There's nothing good that I can see. There's an illness in the air, and all I want to do is erase the part of me that feels. It's selfish, isn't it? I'm surrounded by destruction yet all I think about is how to fix my faults. I've been alone for some time, and when distractions barely work, my mentality declines. I throw my dignity aside and welcome darkness by my side. It's always been a problem. I scratch at my existence just to find a purpose. Am I fine or am I falling far behind? I can barely tell the difference. I stay away from human interaction, and maybe that's the reason why I feel so fucking distant. I barely remember what day it is, let alone the month. Everything feels rapid when all I do is wake up to disaster and sleep within a restless slumber. Time is such a hurtful concept. I've learnt that it has to be accepted, but what if I refuse to? What if I feel as though my minutes have been wasted? They've somehow turned to years, yet I stand here still imperfect.

Papikins

Epsilon

You lied to me. You made me believe that love existed. I gave you a part of me which no one ever knew. I let you in when I was scared, and I hoped you'd love me too.

Papikins

Self-made poetry

I miss the way we used to be, when we were lighting up the skies with self-made poetry, but now I'm here alone composing heartless symphonies. I'm adjusting to life without you, however hard that it may be. There's an emptiness inside me, and it never seems to sleep. I find myself in places that I never wished to seek. There are times when these words collide without a sense of symmetry. I recall the years we were together, but that's a distant memory. I just hope you're doing well without me.

My forever

I remember you. You were my forever. You were the croaking in my throat, and the air that filled my lungs. You were the picture I once held when I walked into the cold. You were my everything. Love is made to be unkind. We bring each other up until the darkness washes every bit of happiness away. I would stare at you for as long as I could, just to get lost within your eyes. You were my home. I sometimes wonder where I'd be if I never fell in love. Where would I be if there was no us? I saw the universe behind your eyes, yet little did I know that our planets would collide. I miss what we had, but I need to keep it quiet. I don't regret you. I don't regret our time together. I just wish it could have been forever. You've always been a part of the words I try to hide, but when I find myself alone, I whisper all the moments that we shared in life. I hate that you're a secret now when you used to be the reason why I smiled.

Do you remember me? I was your forever. I was the warmth behind your skin, and the touch that gave you safety. I was the light behind your rain when you wanted to wash away the pain. I was yours completely, but our love decayed. If I had known our history would one day fade, I would have tried to make you stay. We can never see into the future, and I never thought I'd see a day where all I have is me. I needed you. My walls were caving in, and you were all that I could see. We never had the chance to write our story. We never set the stage to go for glory. I would lay there in the dark, wondering how we lost our spark. You were the unsent letters in my mind that never made it out alive. You stringed my thoughts together, and even after all this time, I still remember you as my forever.

When the love we have to give becomes too much of a burden, we refuse to throw it out into the fire. We want to make amends, but we're far away from what we once desired. It's sad, isn't it? We would rather stay than let each other fade. The problem with staying is that we leave our love to hope, and in the end, we're gripping on to a splitting rope. We push and we pull, but eventually it snaps and leaves us further than before. You were my forever. You were the most beautiful and challenging person that I've known, but as I drifted further from the thought of you, I knew. I knew that I loved you. It's strange how one letter could change the meaning of forever. I was endlessly searching for ways to keep us held together, but all I ever did was tear apart our magic. I was begging for you to see me. I just wanted you to notice, but you were blind to all of my advances. You may have been what I saw as my forever, but now that you're gone, you're someone I'd rather not remember.

Papikins

Ghosts

We use each other. It's the saddest truth when it comes to friendship and disaster. We feel like we owe each other more than we can give, but in the end, one only seems to leave. I've wondered why we become attracted to those around us. Could it be their charm? Maybe it's their presence. They make us feel as though we're real, and that's what gives us power. We've been searching for connection for so long, and when we find it, we reach out for the stars. We do everything we can to make each other happy, but with happiness comes pain. We become too attached, too soon. We try to fill these empty spaces to heal a lifetime of intrusions. Peace has always been a part of us, but throughout the years, it's become familiar with being threatened.

There are so many words we leave unsaid when dealing with our friends. We're afraid to give them reasons to cut away our strings. We avoid noticing the pain just to stay the same, but when we bottle up our anger, our friendship only fades. We jump towards conclusions, and we assume the worst to happen. We're incapable of holding on to what we had. When you separate two souls, time is what kills the vibe. You must have felt it too. You must have wondered why you no longer speak to the people you once knew. We're merely lost out in the universe, trying to find pieces that'll fit. It's hard, isn't it? We come together and build towards the future, but suddenly our paths divide when distance disconnects us. The pandemic has shown me that only few are truly there. We're a lonely type of species. We want the world to notice when we're breathing, but when we feel neglected, we detach from those we cared for deeply. It hurts to know that we'll never be the same again, but we lose control over what we call pretence. We wonder why we weren't enough to make them stay, and if they think of us wherever they may be. We crave to be remembered, because that's the only way we'll be proud of what we're worth. It's traumatic, isn't it? We fall into a cycle of wanting to be kept rather than discarded.

I knew distance was a part of letting go, and with every goodbye that never happened, the more I felt alone. We attempt to right our wrongs when we have no idea where we are. We think and we think until we're lost among the stars. There's never a moment where we stop thinking. We repeat our history as we pace towards community. We want to rule the world, so we find others to join us in the experience. The problem is, we find nothing more than sadness. We attach ourselves to faces, but they become names which never served a purpose. We just want to feel alive. We want to raise our hands in hope and survive within temptation. It's greed, isn't it? We chase happiness without understanding what it is, and as the journey moves ahead, we lose the ones we would have died for. It's such a terrible declaration. We only choose to die for people to show our admiration, but they're only words which reduce our distance. We would do anything to keep them here beside us, even if we have to lie. I never thought of myself as a liar until the pieces started to connect. I was lying to myself about the role I played to others. I wanted to be important, but like all things in life, our time together ended without warning.

The stories we live will forever be bittersweet in nature. We give everything we have to show our worth to others. I swear to God it hurts to feel neglected. I've never felt enough. It's a sad truth I've somehow come to terms with. Strangers are the reason we fall apart. They come into our lives and shine a light on where we're standing. We crave to be alive. It's sad, isn't it? We dream of who we are in the arms of someone else, yet we never know what it means to be alone. I've met countless friends before, and many have turned to ghosts. I was lost inside the moment, as I gave them what they wanted. There are those who give and those who take, but the truth is, all of us feel the same. We're scurrying to keep our peace, and as we give and take, we distract ourselves from being. We use each other in our time of need, yet in every story that we tell, the other person is to blame for what we've felt. We're incapable of being honest, and the more we lie, the more we stay the same. It's the distance that ruins what we have, because if neither of us can create pretence, we have no reason to stay as friends.

We hold each other in high regard, mostly based on who we are. But who are we? We're never the same person when blending in with others. We show ourselves in pieces, and our true self is reserved for those we feel are worthy. We can't pretend when we're locked away from friends. We can't choose the words to say, so we go quiet, and the silence pushes us to death. The ones we interacted with in person suddenly turn into a burden. The truth is, we let

36

Papikins

loneliness drive us when connecting with other people. It's how we avoid ourselves. We drift around the universe, hoping to be saved. We give our trust to anyone who's close enough to reach. We're stupid when we're lost. We carry ourselves without any sort of dignity, as we latch on to imperfect souls to cure our hatred for humanity. The more alone I felt, the more I wanted to belong. I wanted to cover up my scars and learn to let others in while I was running from my fears. I never knew how destructive it could be, and how every person that I'd meet would one day harm my peace.

We somehow feel safe when we connect with someone else. We think we found the perfect fit, but we never fear the worst will happen. We're trapped with a false belief they'll stay beside us. Maybe we're gullible. Maybe we would rather be optimistic about the future, but if we have no fear, the inevitable hits us harder. We're logically flawed when we're screaming out to be somewhere close to someone else. We hide the truth in numbers. We never question why we refuse to see red flags, or why we have this need to stay the course in friendship. We don't owe each other anything, yet we assume that connection is infinite. Nothing in this world is certain, not even the bond you form within the present, because the past was surely different, and the future is infectious. We hold on for too long. We want to make it work, but the truth is that it won't. We lose each other instantly, even if it took years to build our history. The future infects us without warning, and when we come full circle, we find ourselves alone again. We want to feel safe in the loving arms of others, but they only damage what little trust we could have given.

We beg to stay the same, but if we refuse to change, we lose respect for what we were. The darkest hours are the ones where we call out to the cold, but all the faces that we knew have only turned from something new to something old. It's the blue, isn't it? We fall between the spaces that we borrowed, as we try to stay on paths we should have never followed. The problem is, we stand in unity until all we have are memories. It's as if we disappear entirely, but when we find each other once again, all we have is silence and a chapter left unwritten. We blame each other for what happens, not realising that every outcome is the same. We connect and we part ways. I realised I shouldn't fear to disconnect when I've lived it more than once. I wanted to know why people leave, but it's only part of life. We can't keep pretending that what we have is what we need, because sometimes, letting go is the only way to be complete.

Papikins

Zeta

You tore me into pieces when I was at my weakest.

Papikins

Eta

You were every missing piece I thought I'd never find. You were the space between my lips when the words 'I love you' crept out from within.

Papikins

Theta

We rarely get the ending we deserve.

Papikins

Valentine

We've grown apart from friendship, and I want to feel you closer. I want to part your lips with mine and get a taste of happily ever after. I want you to be my Valentine. I want you to let me in and give me everything. I want to steal away your agony and replace it with something close to clarity. I want you to fall in love with me. It's been a few years and I feel like you're the one. You give me butterflies whenever I see your wicked smile. It hides the truth from wandering eyes, but in all honesty, your lies are still sublime. You're my fantasy. You're the dream I want to bring to life, because when I'm standing next to you, we're the only ones around. I think about you more than I would like, and I guess it's the reason why I want you to be mine.

I've never let myself fall this hard before, or maybe I have and I'm just a liar. It truly doesn't matter, because I feel like we'd fight the world forever. I want to gaze into your soul and find you before you get the chance to find yourself. It's the moments that I cherish, and if I could hold you for just one second, I think we could have it all. You're beautiful and it's contagious. It's why I'm drawn to you. I'm helplessly in love with what you do to me. You somehow bring me back to life when I feel as though I've died. It's distracting from all the pain I've tried so hard to hide. I'm incomplete without you. It's as if heaven sent an angel to save me from my hell. I have a fear of losing you, because I may somehow lose myself. You're the only one who understands me. I'm attracted to your empathy. It's as if you somehow hold the key to unlock the deepest side of me.

You make me feel as if I'm worthy to love again, even though I'm afraid to give away my trust. I'm addicted to your demeanour. I've seen a side of you which I'm craving to explore. I want to know what makes you tick and what music makes you feel like nothing else exists. I want us to be lost together. I want to give you everything and nothing all at once. I want to surrender to these thoughts of us. You're the only one in colour, and I want to know exactly why. I want to feel you close to me, as I set my soul on fire. I want to burn it all away so we can share the pain. I want you to notice what I'd do for you, because sometimes, I have nothing else to say. You're driving me insane.

I have this need to know you on a deeper level, and I'm sure we'll go together like the devil goes with hell. It may be doom and gloom, but I'm tired of trying to stay away from evil. I want you to give me a chance to show you that I'm stable. I'd give anything to make you mine, even if it means to carve your name into my skin. You'd be the art behind my sin, and I wouldn't think twice before laying down the ink. You're beautifully designed, and I feel like we'd be atrociously imperfect. I may be pessimistic, but it's a part of why I'm surrounded by enchantment. I'm unable to see beauty in humanity, but when I'm lost inside your eyes, I can see eternity. I want this story to last until the end of days. I want you to believe in me when I'm tired of keeping faith. I need you to be my Valentine, if only for just one day.

Papikins

Succubus

I thought you were the one. I pushed aside my fears to give you what you want. You were feeding off my heart like a succubus. You had your hands around my neck but I still stayed to somehow feel enough. I buried what we lost and don't want to dig it up. All I have to say is goodbye to the one I used to love.

Iota

We were what I call perfect, but I'm glad we ended. It takes courage to be able to let go. I wanted to force us back into existence, but I knew we would have never lasted. I'd rather enjoy the moments that we had than try to recreate the past.

Kappa

I'm afraid of the sun. I'm afraid of being burnt by only just one touch. I don't want to be close to the unknown when the ground I'm standing on doesn't feel like home.

Papikins

Me, myself, and I

We never truly know exactly who we are, and we shy away from understanding why we're flawed. I always wondered why I've felt alone, and why I can't find myself even when I try. I'm scared of what I'll see when looking deep into my eyes. I don't want to ruin my perception of who I am inside. I have a problem with not loving my imperfections. I really hate to see them, but they corner me when I'm overthinking. It's the thinking that breaks apart my sanity. I'd rather erase the person that I used to be than stand here repeating history. It's a shame we can't forget, but to forget is somewhat of a tragedy. You see, our stories intertwine, as we fill our chapters with strangers who somehow turn to lovers. The truth is, they come into our lives to leave. I blame myself whenever I'm left behind. It's my insecurity that ruins me.

I've never been close to perfect, and I don't think I'll ever be enough to say it. It's how the world has treated me. They disregard potential and want me to be beautiful. I don't believe that beauty can hide my imperfections, because I see them when looking out into the distance. The truth is, I feel too much, yet I never feel enough. I'm tired of people telling me to love myself when I can't even stare into the mirror for longer than five seconds and see nothing but sad eyes and a smile that's carved into my face. I do it to myself, don't I? I set unrealistic expectations of how I should look and act based on what I see around me. I want to be a perfect person, but perfection is non-existent. Nothing truly exists. We shape words around lies created by influential minds. I'm sick and tired of feeling inadequate the more I come to age. The harsh truth is that beauty is associated with youth, but I'm still a beautiful creature who deserves some kind of praise.

I've tried to calm the monster that's inside me, but it hurts to be alone. I'd rather have it here beside me, as I lose myself entirely. How can I define myself when others do so freely? I don't want to manifest a word into existence, because I've never claimed to practice sorcery. We want to find escape outside our shared reality. We want to dream about the future, but if we never run, we'll stay within our boundaries. I'm tired of all the misery. I'm tired of seeing pictures of what we should aspire ourselves to be. Is it healthy? Is it truly what drives us in humanity? To attain a perfect face or a perfect body? To unlock potential in our minds from those who are driven by their gluttony? It's greed, isn't it? We want to be recognised so badly that we hurt others in the process.

I realised I was dismissive when it came to what's in front of me. I felt afraid of who I am, but more afraid of what I'd eventually become. I was vulnerable yet I played the victim well. The problem with vulnerability is that I was targeted by white lies and pretty faces. I just didn't want to feel alone. I would do anything to feel connected. I would disregard the tension in my chest and the discomfort in my gut. I thought I could be wanted, but I only detached from who I was. We vie to stay relevant when our reasons to live are miniscule. I kept searching, and I kept searching, but all I ever found were worthless promises. We pledge the world to one another just to feel a sense of safety. It's disgusting, isn't it? We want to find someone to share our troubles with, but they soon become a part of what we hated. I always find myself losing self-respect whenever I'm the only one who's left.

I always seem to have a problem with understanding what I'm worth. I'm scared of being happy when I feel as if it's forced. It's just a word. Everything is just a word, and these words are what deplete my energy. They cross my mind in synergy, as I comb through time and what it did to me. It's the world. It's every distraction I'm attached to. I seem to become addicted to whatever reaches for my soul, even if it's not good for me at all. Am I afraid to smile because it hurts? Am I afraid to lean towards dishonour in case my honesty is ruined? I tried my best to make others see themselves, but the truth is, I never thought about myself. I lied through my fucking teeth to create a loving gaze. I don't want to be tied to love forever. I don't want to burn the image in my head and go in circles once again. Loss is a part of love, and when we lose in love, the pain extends to self. I fell deeper into madness, as I fled across the skies to ask someone for forgiveness.

I can never seem to forgive myself. I argue in my head with the thoughts that cut my breath. I want to be a better person, but when it comes to honour, I'm a criminal at best. It's tragic, isn't it? I've learnt to hate myself the most when I'm crushed by the tension in my chest. We view others so differently compared to how we view ourselves. We wish the best for everyone, but secretly want them all to fail. It's toxic, isn't it? The comparisons we draw are how we lose our friends. We thought they'd never change, but no one ever stays the same. It's how we go our separate ways. We deny that growth is part of life, and we envy joy if it isn't by our side. I always believed people would stay by me forever, but as time went by, hundreds came, but only few remained. It's how we move from place to place. We travel far and wide, and the faces turn to names. We're left alone with thoughts that bring us tears when said aloud. We wonder why we were never good enough to keep them here. We hate what we've become. We hate the reasons why we can never feel enough, and when it comes to loss, we hate the person we thought deserved our love and trust.

The memories are somewhat haunting. They break me down in stages. It's as if I relive everything when I'm overthinking. I paint a picture in my mind, but it only turns to torture when the memories aren't aligned. It's the problem with being human. We recollect the past, but it's been cut to move too fast. I would always wonder why I'm here, and why the fuck I care. I wanted to understand why I lost my self-belief, but I couldn't see beyond the tired eyes which were glued to my disguise. It's time. It's always time. It changes who we are, as we learn to live with every scar. We move in sync with decrepit stars, but when the stars are dead and gone, we fade into the night. It's beautiful, isn't it? How they sit to illuminate the skies until they lose their shine. We take everything for granted, not realising that it's all connected. We're the stars who sit quietly at night, with heads as heavy as the rain. We desperately try to find our light, but our thoughts only lead us towards pain.

The sad reality of loneliness is that it's hard to be explained. It tears us up inside until we lose trust in who we are. It's hard to be left alone when carrying endless scars. My heart is prone to breaking, and when I failed in love, reality was shaken. I couldn't recognise exactly who I was. It's the death of love that causes a surprise. I was nowhere near as complete as I had hoped, and I searched for clarity in quotes. It's what we do whenever we barely understand. We try to calm our nerves through a sentence or maybe two, but it never seems to work. We need more. We need the bitter truth. It was always the same stance—that I was worthy of being loved beyond the love I lost. It's so easy to spread false hope, but to do it so unnaturally was deafening. Maybe I prefer to find the answers for myself. Maybe I need to hear that I'm not perfect, so I won't ever place importance on obtaining what I can never hold. It irritates the fuck out of me to be lost here in the cold.

I'm exhausted of losing sleep over mistakes I made before. I've tried to make amends, but now I'm losing hope. There was a silence in the air, and it followed me wherever I would go. I greeted people I wish I never knew, as I tried to distract myself from what I feel. I wanted to be remembered the way I remember others. I've never had the courage to try to be myself, because when I show that side of me, all the stars are gone. I'm left stranded with my reflection, and I'm far away from the planets I was chasing. We align ourselves with those who somehow fit our lonely universe. We believe they

Papikins

were made for us, but when we crash and burn, our kingdoms turn to dust. We surround ourselves with imitations of who we'd like to be, as we try to mimic what we see. I would always run away from who I am. I was scared of showing wounds from a time I barely understood. I wanted to change myself for the greater good, but when we show discomfort in who we are, we find ourselves at war.

The more I detached myself from what I held inside, the more I felt alone. I could never be content with what I have. It was a part of me I could never stand. We let ourselves go too soon. We're left with thoughts of anguish underneath the moon. We hide away our flaws until we're howling at the skies. We want to be heard, but the truth is, it's only in our minds. We're stuck inside of recurring dreams, because we have no faith in who we are. It's the illusions that hurt the most. We try to lose ourselves in thoughts, but all they do is make us worse. I would close my eyes to be somewhere far from home. I wanted to find sanctuary behind the lies I've told. I've tried to fight the cold, but the silence had evolved. I always thought it was against me, but truth be told, it's the reason why I'm standing. There have been instances where I drove myself to madness as I fell into distractions, but after all the stars had died, my planets had aligned, and I knew I'd forever have me, myself, and I.

Papikins

Lambda

She hid behind the monsters in her closet, and one by one, they
clawed away at her existence.

Papikins

Mu

My story is unwritten and tomorrow isn't promised, but I know these chapters will guide me to salvation. I wanted to set fire to the world, but I was scared of getting burnt. I'm changing with the seasons, and maybe that's why I'll never find my place. I'm spreading to the masses, but I never feel like I'll connect.

Papikins

My quiet storm

I hate that I love you. I hate everything about this; about us. You make me feel weak, and it doesn't feel like I'm close to fine. The way you put your arms around me sends a chill up and down my spine, like a stranger preying in the night. How did our end transpire? I'm holding on to us, because I'm afraid of feeling lost. I'm afraid of being me without you. I'm afraid to walk alone, knowing that I once had someone to calm my quiet storm. Alas, that's how my story goes. I fall apart whenever I remember that I once called you my home.

Papikins

Hopelessly romantic

When you lose the one you love, you surrender all your strength. You're reminded of the emptiness you shared, and question whether they'll return. They were a part of you, wholeheartedly. They pushed you to follow through with dreams, but now they're gone and you've been thrown across the stream. You see, we're constantly trapped within a sea of thoughts, and when our lives begin to crumble, we find it hard to swim towards the surface. We have a craving to fill our lives with passion. We want someone to show us the meaning behind affection, and believe me, when we find it, it's infectious. We're in love with the idea of being wanted, because we never seem to fit within the silence. We want to find someone to share our burdens with. To love is to be selfish, and to be selfish is to love. We gather everything we have and piece ourselves together. We long for the warmth that's been missing from our skin. It's a toxic way to live. You're drawn to love because of fear. You find it hard to be alone, so you choose someone who'll never feed your soul.

I truly think you're beautiful, but to be honest, you deserve to know the truth. It's reckless to be romantic when all you want is to be noticed. We're hopelessly addicted to the taste of what could be, and we'd do anything to keep our promises. We would lie to one another just to hold on to what we have, but is it love without respect? We're drawn to how it feels to be connected. We never see the truth behind romantic dreams. We fall in love to fill the void, and the more we stay together, the less we stay the same. I kept falling, and I kept falling until the love I had to give remained there without meaning. I was in love with the idea rather than the feeling. It's how we build distractions. We love for wrong reasons, as we're led towards dishonesty and guilt. We lift our mask above our head, and the mirror only shows regret. We live to love, but we never love to live. It's the most heart-breaking realisation that I've come to.

We have a certain pull towards love. It never seems to let us go, and when it comes to loss, we shed tears when we find ourselves alone. The truth is, we never look beyond. We're feeble in our search for love. It's hope, isn't it? We let emotions ruin us. We're grounded by the thoughts of how it feels to find the one. I had always been hopeless when it came to being a romantic. There were thoughts which crossed my mind of how perfect it would be, but I never saw what attachment did to me. I was focused on being better, not only for myself, but for someone else. I would only seem to lose what I had before and set the stage for something new. It's a side of me I wish I never knew. I long to find my missing pieces, but in doing so, I'm left wondering what I'm worth. I've always had a problem with imperfection, and when I'm not as valued as I hoped, it only makes me worse. It's what love does to me. I want to change myself so I can finally show the world I'm not as hopeless as I thought.

We tend to fall in love when we barely feel enough. It's what I did when I was craving to be noticed. I wanted to be alive within the universe, but I only led myself to ruin. We always fear to be held,

Lovedemic

because eventually those arms will disappear within the silence. We remember names, but throughout the years they become a pain to mention. It's as if we repeatedly push towards the sun and wonder why we burn. It's love, isn't it? We want it to fit the narrative, but nothing comes together quite rapidly as love and loss in their entirety. We feel like we have time, but the clock is unforgiving. It pushes us towards the end, and suddenly, we're alone and reliving all our memories. It's a reminder of how human we can be. I wanted to taste the future on someone's lips, but I only got a glimpse of agony. I can't seem to grasp what's wrong with me. I fight for love like it's my calling, but when I get attached, it feels as if I'm falling.

I'm cursed as fuck and out of luck. I love for selfish reasons so I can feel enough. I can barely trust myself when it comes to what I want. I'm afraid of where I'll be if I carved another name into my heart. It's poetic, isn't it? We would desecrate ourselves to prove how dedicated we can be, but that's part of why we're thrown away. We give too much and expect little in return, even when there's nothing truly there. I would create a perfect love affair and wander into thoughts of how beautifully chaotic it would be to push aside my sadness and live within a dream. I'm hopelessly romantic, but the world has only thrown me into madness. I've never felt enough, not even when in love. I thought it could be perfect, but after every echo in the silence, what happened to my mind was only tragic.

I would stare at my reflection and wonder why it felt so distant. It was my eyes which made little sense at all. They told a story which I barely had the strength to share. I would look close enough to see

Papikins

my imperfections. I wanted to understand the difference between love and indecision. I had always wanted to be connected, but I couldn't. I was afraid that I'd be seen behind the mask I'm wearing, and I truly hated what's in front of me. It's heartbreak, isn't it? We love just enough to tear ourselves apart. I wanted to find relief from the painted smile that rested on my face. It was a part of me which I wanted to erase. I sometimes found myself alone, wondering who I am behind the constant screaming in my head. I was helplessly addicted to whatever silence I could find, as I sat and contemplated why I felt indifferent. It was peace for me. I couldn't stop myself from thinking, but in the space between fiction and reality, I found a sense of safety.

I saw no end to what I felt. It lingered in my head, as I tried to force myself to forget. There's no running from the past. No matter how many times we close our eyes, the memories remain intact. I know how you feel, and like I said, you're beautiful. It's just a part of life which no one can ignore. I based my healing on empty quotes. I would stare at all the words, yet they barely gave me hope. It's poetry, isn't it? We aim to connect in such few lines, but some are only filled with lies. They illustrate what it means to love, but the bitter truth is hidden from our fragile eyes. We lose ourselves so quickly, as we try to cover up our scars. We have to be reminded of how beautiful we are, but we're vulnerable enough to believe that we should continue chasing stars. It's misdirection, isn't it? We hide away from truth so we can pretend what we had was wrong. It's hard, you know? We want the world to stop, because we feel like we've failed in love. I always wanted to remove what I felt before, but to be honest, it would have made me worse.

There's nothing to forget. There's nothing to regret. We build upon the moments until they're scattered in the wind. They become a part of who we are, even if it felt like hell to be torn apart. I was hopelessly romantic, as I tried to fill this part of me I hated. I wanted what I saw in movies, but the difference is, we rarely have a chance to write our stories with any form of structure. We're incapable of being perfect. There's a fine line between being hopeless and romantic, and I only seemed to fill the role of hopelessness. It's as if I was destined to be vacant. It's tragic, isn't it? I wanted to fill the deepest part of me, but I only dug further into misery. We have an undying need to be whole, but some of us are left with wanting more. The truth about being hopelessly romantic is that everywhere you look, you're reminded of why you're lonely. You wish to fit between the spaces, but they only pull themselves away from where you're standing. I saw what love had done to me, and I knew I had to find myself inside the silence. We neglect ourselves too much when it comes to love. We feel less because of loss. The truth is, no matter how we feel, or how many times we fall apart, we'll always be enough.

Papikins

Another day, another lie

Another day, another lie, another reason why we hurt ourselves at night. We repeat the same words inside our heads, searching for an ounce of happiness. We love, we lie, and we leave. It's as if we're made for this. We avoid the truth because we love the taste of emptiness. We want to fill our veins with fabrications and despair. We're the worst of humanity. We seek for more than air, because we're breathless without attention. We fill our thoughts with promises that are never kept, but to what end? We're heading for disaster when we know the truths are all unsaid.

Stardust

I stare blankly at the moon, as I search for all the stars at night. I wonder how they shine when some of them have died. I'm stuck here underneath their lustrous lights, as I conjure up these thoughts of life. It's a never ending stream of what is and what never had the chance to be. I'm reminded of the love I left behind and the friends I could never keep within my mind. They were once mine, but had faded along with time. We were the stars inside my universe. We were bright, beautiful, and blind. We gave away our sadness to lift each other up, but we were somehow misaligned. I regret the solace we created. It's gone and I'm standing here deluded. I miss the way we were, because all that's left is stardust and seclusion.

Papikins

Disappear

I'm on a path of self-destruction. I want nothing more than to disappear at this very moment. I feel so fucking disconnected from everyone around me, and it doesn't help that I can't talk to people openly. I'm afraid that I'll infect them with depression, because the way my mind is right now is fucked beyond belief. I feel alone. I feel like I'm a burden to people that I'm with. I try to go out to numb this feeling, because I'm scared to be here by myself. I don't want to lay in the dark for hours, feeling lost and damaged. I don't know what to do anymore. Maybe one day this will all fade, and I really do hope so, because I hate everything about my existence.

My existence

I'm fighting with my thoughts and my existence. I'm crying out for help at every instance. I'm falling further from my dreams and aspirations, and I'm torn between the distance. I've had days of overthinking, yet all these thoughts are slightly more depressing. I fall within temptations of being somewhat close to happy, but I'm still afraid of disconnecting. I've been coasting through a life of misdirection, as I search for peace within these empty situations. I'm craving to find acceptance, but I'm only warding off my lonely demons.

Temporary

I've been learning to distance myself. I don't want to be put into a position where I miss someone else's presence. This is the best way to live. I stopped seeing the good in people. There is no good. It doesn't exist in the world anymore. Everyone hides behind a mask. There's no point in searching for meaning. That's all I ever looked for. I wanted to find people who helped me understand who I am, but now I'm finding it hard to connect. Everyone is temporary, including me. I'll repeat it in my head a thousand times over until it's something I believe.

Papikins

Remembered

I have this need to be remembered, and it only makes me worse. I want to be somebody else, because quite clearly, being me is just a curse.

Papikins

A tale of abuse

We wonder what would happen if we meet by chance and share the sadness that life has brought us, but what we fail to see is the wolves who hide their teeth. She was on a search for happiness, like most of us will be. She had never fit within reality, so she tried to live in dreams. The loneliest people are the ones who want to breathe. They place themselves with others to get a glimpse of what could be, but when their voice is quiet, they hardly find relief. There were times where she hid behind her words, but her expression would always tell the truth. She wasn't a lost cause, but she was judged by all her flaws. It's as if people were made to be unkind. They would belittle her existence, yet never wondered why she could barely form a sentence. She was blind to true intentions, and that's why she let her guard down when she met him. She wanted to be more trusting, and she swore she would find someone she could share her life with. It's the story of love that prevents us from being content with standing here alone.

Her eyes were so expressive, yet she never saw people for what they were. She sat away from others, yet close enough for him to touch. He was attracted to her silence, and he couldn't get enough. It's how the wolves will find you. They prey on those who can barely trust themselves. She was awkward and he knew the words to say to give her comfort, but they were painted with dishonesty. It's what some will do to shine a light above their sins. He was never looking for a place to stay, whereas she required haven from the demons which would taunt her. He gave her what she needed, but only for some time. He listened to her grief and gave her loving eyes. It was his dark gaze which she was drawn to. It made her believe that he was different, when in reality, he was just another villain. He gave her hope they'd be together, but all he wanted was to feed into addiction. He wanted to control her, and it's what happens, isn't it? We give ourselves away just for someone else to break.

He held her through her coldest nights, as he gave her peace of mind. He was what she needed at the time. His touch was better than the warmth of the sun, because it made her feel connected. She saw heaven in his smile, but failed to see the hell that he would hide. The trouble with wolves in disguise is that they keep you satisfied until they greet you by surprise. The love he had to give was never worth the amount that she believed, yet he made it seem as though it's perfect. He knew how to be supportive, as he moved her away from everybody else. She was isolated to ensure he would get his way. It's how he stalked his prey. He wanted to be the only one she could confide in, even if he was never made to stay.

She felt her heart was growing, and her chest could hardly contain the love she felt for him. He was sweet. He was sincere. He was seductive. It's a shame he used emotion to provoke such beauty into submission. He hid behind his mask, pretending to be another person. He would softly whisper lies into her ear to have her where he wanted. She never felt as though she's good enough, but when

Papikins

she stood beside him, she felt the world was hers. Sadly, it's how protection creates affection. He was calculated beyond her recognition. His words were so ill-fitting, yet she fell for his delivery. They filled her head with joy, but when the time would come, he would take it all away. He was a master of deception, and he knew he could always make her stay. It was as if he found pleasure in how her happiness decayed. He kept her close enough to hold, yet little did she know, she was another puppet in his show.

The days would pass, and he would slowly start to change. He was growing restless of being there beside her. He never intended to stay for long, but the more she gave into his demands, the more reason he had to shy away from what he planned. He would undermine her worth, and ask her why she wore a certain style of clothes. He didn't want anyone to notice her. He would shout in anger, as he threw around his words. The labels would keep appearing, and she felt restricted to be human. He was vicious. He was vulgar. He was violent. He would apologise when his hands would harm her, but she was scared of rejecting his insincerity. She didn't want to believe her beloved was anything less than what she previously envisioned.

She would wait for him outside, and he would barely be on time. She wondered where he was, and if she should stay for hours in the cold. He gave her nothing in return, yet she tried to give him all her best. He would finally appear with faint lipstick stains across his neck. The truth is, she didn't dare to question where he'd been. She didn't want to be alone again. She felt his arms around her, and she knew he was the one who ruined the castles that she built. It's the first realisation that hits the hardest. She still tried her best to hide it, but how long can a person keep pretending? How long until the days were only meant for nothing? It's stories like these that are hard to properly convey, but to be blind and say they don't exist, is to cower from the pain. She may have been afraid, but the fire had awoken. It was somewhere deep inside, waiting to one day find the light.

She was still wrapped around his finger, and he took advantage of her loyalty. She was stuck inside of his embrace, but she knew exactly who he was when looking at his face. He was a monster. He was a part of her destruction, and the sad truth is, she was still in love with him. She was simply trying to make it work, but deep down, she knew it never would. It's the problem with trying to fix whatever shit that we've been given. We stay, and we stay but for what reason? It's the days that keep repeating, but we age, and we age until time is gone and we're stood in silence with a frozen heart. He sat beside her in her darkest hours. She appreciated everything he did, but his deception left a mark on the lies she once believed.

He pushed her towards the edge, as he hid behind of his affairs. He knew she wouldn't leave, but that's the problem with humanity. We disregard insanity. We disregard that making the same mistakes repeatedly will surely ruin us entirely. She was shamed. She was scorned. She was strong. They were never her mistakes. She had always blamed herself for the person she'd become, but she finally saw that placing blame on situations is never a part of growth. Her mind was rushing with his empty promises. She was tired of staying still. She had to get away. She could endlessly wonder where she'd be, but the thoughts would never take her out of where she was. There comes a time where we have to push what we want into reality rather than keep holding on to words that float freely through our minds. She had to take action and leave her toxic love behind.

There are those who love and those who taint. She fell in love with lies, and he tainted her with an empty life. She couldn't stand the screaming. She couldn't keep pretending that it was right to be abused. He continued to shout until the bitter end, but he never realised how bright her fire burned. She was done with feeling insignificant. She was done with being disrespected. She had to run from the life she never wanted, and she never dared to question why she gave his name to be reported. It's courage, isn't it? She had lived through hell for so long without knowing it was wrong. She would stare at every single mark against her skin, and every thought he planted in her head. She was scared she could never find herself again. She was lost and she was damaged, but the words that were left unspoken were the ones which kept her sane. She had to rebuild the sanctuary she once had. It may take time to follow through with change, but a warrior like her always finds their way back into the fray.

Lonely Island

I'm stranded on a lonely island, where dreams are left to die in.

Papikins

Familiar faces

There are no rules to friendship. We seamlessly interact and suddenly we become attached. We want to fight the world together, but we lose track of where we're going. We're alive yet lost. We're the polaroid's and sunsets which were carved into our minds. We hold beliefs that we'll never leave each other's sides. Is it wrong? Is it truly wrong to be caught up in pretence? The truth with friendship has always been the same. The familiar faces fade away, and it hurts like hell when you're the one who still remains. I thought there was something wrong with me. I thought the colours disappeared because I felt too empty. I had to open up my eyes and understand humanity. The sad truth is, all the people that I've met will one day be memories in my head.

Papikins

Depression

I had a thousand dreams but they somehow turned to silence. I had this need to be adored. I had this craving to be seen. I wanted someone to break apart my walls and help me find release. We become addicted to distractions. I would lose myself in words, trying to fix my problems within quotes. The more I inked my misery, the more I'd alter poetry. It's a talent yet a curse, and what's worse is that I barely feel anything at all. These emotions turn to letters and I discard them without thinking. The sad truth has always been that I rarely feel alive. I put myself in situations to bring my story back to life, but I instantly fall into regret and try to hide. It's depression, isn't it? It grabs on to your throat and restricts the air you breathe. You gasp for help but never find relief. It's always had a hold of me, but I never wanted to admit I wasn't normal. I didn't want others to see me at my weakest, so I hid beneath a broken smile. I had to be defensive, in case the world around me crumbled. We only have ourselves in the end, and I had to understand the reasons why I hurt.

There was something I was missing, and it clearly made me uninspired. I would look for beauty all around me, but the colours were too dull to even see. It's as if my world had faded, and the universe had left me in a place where nothing had existed. I was lost inside my head, as the thoughts of love and loss began to cut into my heart. The saddest truth is, my blood was turning blue, because the cold merged into the dark. I was visually impaired by the constant strain of trying to be perfect. I just wanted to belong, but as the days turned into darkness, my thoughts shifted into madness. I was my own worst enemy. I was the villain to my story. I blamed myself for what I've done and couldn't let go of what was wrong. It's how I tried to cope while knowing I was far away from happiness. I wanted to find myself beyond this tragic mess, but depression held me tightly like a corset on a dress.

It's always been about redemption. I thought if I could fix my wrongs, I'd be a better person. The truth is, life is made to bring us down. We look for happiness whenever no one is around, but we run from everything we know. We run far away from future goals we never set, because we were busy chasing happiness instead. I didn't want to be that person. I didn't want to walk along the edge. I wanted to be closer to emotions that I'm missing. I wanted to connect the piece that none of us can truly ever find. It's always there. It's inside all of us. It was the silence screaming back at me. It pulled me on a leash, and I couldn't seem to cut away its strings. I fought a war within my mind. I was tired of letting all these thoughts consume me. I wanted to escape. I wanted to experience the world rather than go back to where I was. It's emptiness, isn't it? The truth is, we're never truly empty. We're suppressing how we feel inside. We don't want to be vulnerable. We don't want to stand still and feel like we've lost our soul. It's emotion, even if you barely feel it, and if you ever looked closely, you can see it in your eyes. Believe me, I can see it in mine.

Papikins

Break apart at nightfall

I'm your soulmate. I'm the voice inside your head when nothing else exists. It's a shame we're far apart from one another. I want you to open your eyes and see me. I want to build a perfect little story, but I need you to know, you're stuck inside what isn't, and I want to bring you back towards what is. We share the same moments, somehow. I've felt your pain, and I know you're lost. I'm a stranger, but here we are. It's just you and I together, and I sincerely hope you realise where we're heading. I can feel the tingle down your spine, and the numbness in your mind. I want you let me in, one last time. This is for you. It's always been for you. I've pushed aside our differences to show you why I feel imperfect. It's time for me to be honest. My objective has always been to give you closure. Maybe not today, and maybe not tomorrow, but one day when it's least expected. Hopefully, you'll remember me.

I've always had a fixation with wanting to save people. I've thought about the implications time and time again. It's how we cope when losing our self-worth. We attach ourselves to ideas. We let them ruin us. We let the stories unfold before our eyes until there's nothing left but loss. I held the chapters in my hands yet nothing seemed to calm the void inside my heart. Nothing ever feels enough, not even success. Are we destined to be dissatisfied with what we've taken? You see, we're never given anything in this world, other than the chance to expose the truth completely. We strive to reach perfection, but rarely see ourselves as worthy. We tempt fate with hidden secrets, as we shy away from honesty. We've never been the type of creatures to let emotions out in their entirety. It's as if we're staring at the sun and our eyes are always closed. We're drawn to darkness, even when the light is shining through.

We search for meaning, and when it's hard to find, we create nothing more than lies. The narrative has always been intriguing. We're curious to know where the answers lie. We want to know our history, and if we'll fit in a different place and time. We have this need to belong, but when our self-belief is shattered, we tend to lose our smiles. I just wanted someone to notice when I'm there, but no one seemed to care. I had little roads to take, so I attached myself to pain. I just wanted to feel something other than mundane. The truth is, I tried to find acceptance while I was hurting, but only found myself trapped among wolves in sheep's clothing. I could never be saved when I was careless. I was pulled back into the fray when I needed to escape. I was weak. I was human. I sat still on a ship that was slowly sinking, but I never realised I was the source of all my problems. I was caught up in trying to be a perfect person, but like many before me, I failed to reach what I expected.

I had a dream where I found perfection inside of someone else. I wanted to learn to love another when I could barely love myself. I had an obsession with connection, and it somehow influenced my ill decisions. I was addicted to letting others ruin me, because my value had depleted. There was a void inside my heart, and I thought I could fill it with true love, but I found it hard to trust. It took me a while to build my walls, and I was scared to break them down. The troubling aspect of love is that it slowly changes who you were. I had closed myself entirely, but I was drifting from place to place to find a glimpse of hope. Lies became a part of how I coped, but nothing hurt as much as how I lowered my self-worth. I wanted to believe that someone out there could be mine. It's loneliness, isn't it? We'd do anything to cure it, but what's left is a broken soul who can't commit. You see, we create our own destiny, but as we move along the future, we somehow forget our basic needs.

We shape ourselves based on who we meet, but never realise who we are. The saddest stories are told by those who smile. I would paint my lips with glee to cover up my misery. It's how I defended myself from all these ghosts I knew before. I would rather be seen as happy than be asked what's wrong with me. It's never an easy question for us to answer. We feel certain emotions which translate so tragically, and sometimes, we're unable to find the words that give them clarity. It's the reason why none of us will ever understand each other. We may share the world together, but we hide our true intentions. The truth is, I've always felt alone, but when the darkness comes, I feel the tension piercing through my bones. I feel a side of me that no one would ever want to know. It's overthinking, isn't it? We find ourselves ensnared in moments we once lived, or future struggles we may face.

We build ourselves from nothing, and suddenly hate what we've become. I've always been the villain, but somehow others see me differently. They may be lying, or maybe I want to believe I'm right. We disregard the ones around us, because we've slowly lost our trust. We'd rather see our faults than find acceptance. But the problem is, we crave to be accepted. How can we find it if we never believe in words that are meant to give us strength? I've lost myself on occasion. I couldn't stop myself from breaking. It's hard to carry on when you barely feel alive. You wonder why you're empty, and why the sunrise has turned to night. You sleep away the sadness, but it's always on your mind. You'd give anything to find peace, but you know surrendering would only cause more grief. There were days where I could barely breathe. I was drowning without water. I was scared of pushing further. I just needed somewhere quiet to reclaim control of what I've lost.

It takes some time to be able to fulfil what you desire. I felt in dire need of saving, but if I couldn't save myself, I would rather be alone. We place importance on connection. We want to find a home away from home, but when our stories end, it hurts like hell to be back to where we were. I let the thoughts control me. I had to. I let go of everything just to be able to forgive myself for falling. I kept thinking, and I kept thinking until I left behind the person I've become. There's this dream I had of being happy, but there was no happiness inside me. I couldn't find what I was looking for. Did I deserve to chase the unattainable? There was nothing I could do, and I knew it. I realised I would only stunt my growth if I kept my dreams alive. We seem to dream forever until all our time is gone. Some of us will neglect the fact that we've been standing still. It hurts, doesn't it? We wish we could have it all, but as the days turn into years, we break apart at nightfall.

To lose yourself is a beautiful feeling, because you somehow find the hidden views inside your mind. We would rather hide behind dishonesty than show ourselves entirely. I would change myself to stay relevant in other people's lives. I wanted to adapt to my surroundings rather than be the main attraction in my story. The problem is, when we live for others, we rarely get to shine. I was a shadow of my former self, as I followed distractions into what I thought was help. I wanted to get better, and when the night came, it was time to pick apart the ache. It's something many of us refuse to do. We don't want to relive the pain. It's as if we're scared that remembrance will drive us towards insanity, and believe me, it hurts to suddenly rewind. I had to understand the truth behind my lies. There were so many reasons why I cried at night. I thought back at what I had and wondered where the fuck I am. We compare ourselves to who we were, but never understand why we had to change. I was desperately in love with nostalgia, and it was only killing me.

We give too much and expect little in return, but we never give enough to where it's needed. I was focused on being selfless, but never fed my soul in the process. I needed to release these demons, because without any form of closure, I would have never even been here. The hardest thing to accept is how badly you treat yourself, and I was guilty of having no self-worth. It's regret, isn't it? We come to a stage in life where we feel helpless. We keep pushing towards the light, but the emptiness is lingering somewhere out of sight. I had always been afraid of being empty, but I never realised what it truly meant. We feel too much, yet it never feels enough. We become numb, as we frantically search for reasons why we're out here in the cold. I didn't want to be found. I didn't want to be exposed. We live to forgive, but I was tired of forgiveness if it meant I had to forgive myself. We never take the blame completely. We hate ourselves but never learn from our mistakes. I was sick of going nowhere. I knew there was something missing, and I needed the courage to push myself to find it.

We were created with an idea that everything will come together, but what if it doesn't? We're bound to be affected by the truth more than lies. We would rather listen to false hope than to actually understand what it means to be alive. I prayed for life to fill my lungs, but every prayer was left unanswered until I freed my mind. There had always been a tension in my brain. It would tighten up at times until these words would seldom leave. I couldn't handle being thoughtless. I knew I was suppressing more than sadness, but I was scared to open up when all I felt was dead. We reveal so much yet so little when we start to overthink. We want to eradicate our scars yet never try to be accepting. I knew there was more to life than hurt, but if I couldn't trust myself to think, wasn't I already close to death? We bleed into these pages so quickly. It's life, isn't it? We form chapters in our story which only ever haunt us. I was living in regret of what I've done, yet the hardest truth to face was the person I've become. I was never able to think outside the circle, and like I said, if we live for others, we'll never be close to what we feel is fine.

We desperately try to find ourselves in the shadow of our friends and family, as we seek for their approval. It's hard to go unnoticed. The truth is, belonging is like a drug. We're addicted to completion, and when we connect to one another, all our worries slip away and we feel safe. It's a temporary cure to loneliness. We would rather throw ourselves into places which aren't good for us than learn to be alone. There are many people out there who thrive when they're together, but once their enthusiasm expires, they have nothing left but memories. They stand still when their minds are begging them to move. We have to accept that loneliness is a part of life at times, and we should never stop believing in who we are. It's the thoughts that ruin us. We lack the will to love ourselves, and in turn, we lose the energy to focus.

I was too hard on myself. I would wonder why I'm the only one who's left, and if I deserve to suffer in neglect. Maybe it was selfish. We seem to expect too much when it comes to love and friendship, but we forget everyone is the same as us. We rarely want to look at each other the way we see ourselves. We're human and we're flawed. I would sit on trains and buses, and I had no sense of empathy. I thought of everyone as fixtures in my story. It's how we interact with strangers. They could be suffering in silence, just like you and I, but all we do is disconnect from our surroundings. We avoid eye contact because we're afraid of the unknown. I didn't want to be afraid anymore. I didn't want to be selfish. How can I understand the world if I don't see it in its entirety? I only ever thought about myself, and that was almost going to be the death of me. The mind is a strange tool, and most of us are unaware of what we do. We're clueless to what's around us. I had enough of being blind. I had to open up my eyes beyond what I felt inside. It holds us back when we're stuck with feelings of self-pity. I needed to expand my train of thought and break apart at nightfall.

I was gasping for air, but never felt the need to breathe. I knew the pain was self-created, and if I wanted a solution, I had to find release. We sometimes lose ourselves without understanding why. We feel tension in remembrance, and it deters us from digging deeper. I never felt enough, and it truly affected my decisions. I was never sure of where I'm going, and I wanted to be happy, but if I couldn't be happy with myself, why was I searching for someone else? We have to realise that life only hurts if we allow it to. We have to build our strength to fight through storms, and if we fall into the silence, we have to learn to swim towards the surface. I had to stop pretending I had time. The clock would move without me, and all I lost were my surroundings. I couldn't help but notice the more I aged, the more I felt alone. I was searching for the person I was before rather than opening new doors. Loneliness is merely a frame of mind, and what I realised is that if I want the world to see me, I have to make it mine.

Papikins

Magnets

I can't help but stare at the creases in your lips, as we lean in for a kiss. They show the world you've witnessed with a smile that's almost restless. It feels like heaven lost an angel, because your beauty is so timeless. Your aura is electric, and I find myself enchanted. You're my everything. I've said it many times before, but you truly are captivating. Maybe it's that sparkle in your eyes, or the way you wear that beautiful disguise. You make perfection seem effortless, and it's clear that I've lost my senses. You're irresistibly attractive, and I'm drawn to you as if you're made of magnets. I'm afraid of what you do to me. You're increasing my anxiety, and I can see it clearly. Every thought I have is connected to our memories. You're the only one I want. I'm astounded by your touch, because of how cold your fingers are. I know your life's been rough, but you're capable of burning brighter than the stars. I'm amazed by everything you do, and maybe that's the reason why I'm hopelessly drawn to the idea of being close to you.

Loveless

When I saw you for the first time, I could tell our paths would somehow intertwine. You were my light. You got me through the darkest side of life. You were mine. We always assume that people stay, but the reality is, they never do. I remember what it's like to fall in love. I was drawn to the idea of romance. I wanted my worries to slip away, as I fell into another's arms. It's the dream, isn't it? We value ourselves so little that we need someone to remind us that we're worthy. We fall within distractions to calm our souls, but when they leave, heaven turns to hell. I always knew stories came to an end, but I never wanted to admit I had to close the book on ours. I thought the chapters were unread, but it turns out, we had abruptly reached the end. You were my fairy tale, and I wish I never lost a friend. It's love. It comes into our lives and replaces the silence we once felt, but as the days progress, we become detached from the walls that we once built.

We were made to fall in love, but we were also made to tear apart. It's cruel, but life is made to be unkind. We have these empty spaces that are seeking to be filled, and when we fill them, the bottom is left endless. That's how it is to love. You somehow find a purpose to stay through storms that left you restless, but when it's gone, you find yourself more breathless. We can never fill what was, and maybe that's the problem. We're seeking to recreate what used to be rather than living with what is. It's what we do. It's part of

85

humanity that repeats itself in every story. We just want familiar faces to keep us sane within the silence, but they never stay, do they? They're the reason why we ultimately break, and when we break, we find ourselves as loveless.

You never forget what it feels like to be wanted. It's why it's hard to say goodbye, because you're somehow left wondering if it was all a lie. We grow apart. It's what we do. We change our views, and suddenly our paths become unglued. You gave me love. You gave me loss. You gave me hope that tomorrow would be ours. I used to be so hopeless. I used to believe that we'd one day ride towards the skies and live among the stars, but my dreams have only turned to scars. There used to be a light, and no matter how hard I try to lie, I loved the way it shined. The problem is, I never knew that it would burn me. We assume that darkness is the culprit, but our happiness is taken even when we try our best to save it. There are a thousand ways to lose yourself, and love? Love is what we share. It's universal. We build our stories up and break our walls apart. We want to connect, but sometimes, there's nothing left, not even a single thread.

When our love had been erased, I used to love to fall asleep, because I was addicted to my dreams. I would visualise a perfect paradigm of somewhere close to paradise, and you were always by my side. You were close enough to touch, but before I even could, you'd somehow turn to dust. We sometimes forget what we've lost. Our subconscious brings back the familiar feelings, and we miss the warmth of being wanted. We remind ourselves of the past and how

86

beautiful it was. The problem is, it'll never be again. We attach ourselves to ache, and we wonder why we want to stay. The part of life that hurts the most is when it's time to say goodbye. I was avoiding the inevitable. I thought I could bring back what I had, but the sad reality of the past is that it only lingers in your mind. To live within the moment is to live in your entirety, and if you're stuck repeating history, you're as dead as you can be.

We assume that hope will give us what we need, but when we're helplessly hoping for revival, we only smile in dreams. It's remembrance, isn't it? We remember everything, yet we fail to realise that what we had is gone. You see, when we over-feel and over-love, we lose even harder. We search for reasons just to stay, but the person we're holding on to eventually starts to fade. We try to find solutions, but our connection has decayed. We can feel it. We can taste it on their lips every time we kiss. We feel uneasy about the future, because we wonder where we'll be. The truth is, there is no future with the person who turned into your hell. We forget about the chapters. The story never ends until we close our eyes for good, and maybe even then it truly doesn't. You can either repeat the same mistakes, or you can finally accept that even after all the shit you've been through, it's sometimes peaceful to be loveless.

Mine

There were many moments where I felt like I could fly, but the one I'll never forget is being by your side. We would calmly stare into the sea, as the sun rose to bring us light. We shared each other's company, even in our saddest times. It was purely unconditional, and I loved to call you mine.

Papikins

Nu

We threw away forever. We threw away the life we made together, and now what we had is muted down to a dying ember.

Papikins

Ruin me

I want you to ruin me; the way that it's supposed to be. Love me and break me. Take advantage of my insecurities. I want you to make my heart bleed. This is love, isn't it? These are the lies I told myself, as I placed you on a pedestal. We spun around in circles, as our love was dying. The painful truth is, I never saw it coming. I tried to fix the cracks, but you were never eager to. I made excuses to be close to you. We were going nowhere, and in the end, I was the only one who cared.

Ocean full of thoughts

I'm too afraid to love. I'm afraid I'm not enough. These thoughts are driving me insane. Who am I in this world of pain? I keep thinking, and I keep thinking until I overthink. There's an endless ray of hope within this ocean full of thoughts, but do I swim, or do I sink? I've seen these ghosts before within these vacant dreams that hold me still. I lived within the confines of the past. I wanted to fill my head with sorrow, as I neglected the possibilities of tomorrow. The reason why I wanted to be alone was pretty simple. I never knew who to trust or give my heart to. I thought that somehow it would be you. I guess I never got to be your one and only.

The past is unforgettable. I look for all the pieces that I never understood, wishing I could place them somewhere in the blue. It isn't easy being cold and distant. I find myself longing to have purpose, as I try to find connection. I want you to feel me hurting, just so you can see how much I care. I'm lost within these words of beauty and distress, as I cope with everlasting loneliness. I saw the world for what it is, yet these pictures of us are all I'll ever miss.

Papikins

Nocturnal night

Nocturnal nights full of tears and wine. I medicate the demons with spirits stuck inside my system. I want to feel more than human, so I pick up a bottle just to drown out all the screaming. I'm locked in and blacked out. I'm addicted to poison and I can't breathe when I'm sober. I'm just trying to make sense of what caused my affliction, but the past is too blurred when I'm focused on drinking. I think too much and it's surely a problem. I'm reminded of mistakes and I'm still unable to solve them. The nights are so long compared to the morning, or maybe I'm lost in a world of indulgence. I just wish I could stop hearing this silence, because one day I may be brought to the edge, but until then, I'll fight depression with every ounce of my strength.

Papikins

Burn the book

I had a repetition in my head of all the things we ever did and ever said. I was breaking piece by piece, trying to figure out if this was it. I needed something to pull me back towards the surface, because I was drowning in regret. Did we ever have a choice in what was happening to us? Why am I feeling low when all I wanted was to love? Every picture tells a story, and every memory remains. I had you for a while, yet your heart was detaching me with time. I never knew how hard it was to lose, but now I'm back to being one. I hope to God that it was worth it, because I feel as though I'm dying. Every part of me decayed within an empty space, as I felt your presence drift away. I used to feel alive, but now I want to die. All I ever did was try to make you smile. I put my needs aside so you would stay and still be mine. I don't know if it's normal, but I can't remember who I was before you.

The voice inside my head was echoing a note I tried to dispossess. I had to escape from the ideologies of pain. I wanted to be real. I wanted all the lies to be erased. Every ounce of energy I had was slowly fading, as I tried to wash away your bitter taste. I wanted to show the world that I can do this, as I suffered within silence. It was a part of me I hated. I would sit and think about the times we shared rather than find myself again. I was lost in our embrace, but I knew we'd never be the same. We seem to fall to madness when we lose the one we cherished. I wanted to be a better

93

person, and believe me, I tried to be. I tried to change myself entirely. I was too in love with the idea of forever, not realising our end was drawing closer. If only you knew. If only you fucking knew how hard I tried to love you. Maybe we'd be different. Maybe you'd still be here, but I doubt it. I'm tired of being optimistic when all it's ever done is make me feel unwanted.

I knew I was living in the past, yet I had little strength to move. The world kept pushing me away from the moments that we had. The hours would turn into days, as I kept thinking of your face. I had so much left to say, and all I needed was a friend, but I had no one to remove all of my rage. I tried so hard to change myself into someone else. The truth is, there was nothing I could fix. I was too far gone inside of loneliness. I truly wanted to see you happy, but what we had were unkept promises. We were lying to each other to keep what we had together. I sometimes wondered why I felt the way I do, and why I tried my best to forget you. We're sometimes put in a position to be cowards. We want to run from the truth rather than accept it. I couldn't move on if I forgot. I didn't realise how much I'd lag behind, as I thought about our life and the love that died. It's self-destruction, isn't it? We focus on what we shouldn't. We let the days pass with thoughts that only hurt us. There's no need to forget. There's no need to be scared. It took some time to understand how I could move ahead, but when I finally faced the truth, I knew what I had to do.

Everything that happened made me who I am. Everyone I met and lost was an essence of my soul. They were a part of me which I had lived and one day loved, but time is unforgiving. It gives and takes without warning. I know how you feel. Trust me, I do. I've seen love turn into hate, and the world burn before my eyes, as I watched the ones I held close start to fade away. I've been through hell and back to try to shape my future, but everything seemed to bring me back to what I used to have. I was always afraid of saying goodbye, because I didn't want to live in an empty universe for one. I was running from myself. I hated what I saw inside the mirror. I don't remember how it started, but I needed to somehow end it. I had to learn to walk alone again. We never realise how hard it is to stay truthful to ourselves, and when our trust is gone, we're valued less than what we're worth.

When you walk beside someone for so long, you forget the person you once were. You build yourself around the one you love, but that version of you is never someone you should trust. We lie so much. We become too toxic to tell the truth, and honestly, we're unable to be honest when we're on a road to lose. I couldn't push myself to feel. I thought I had to suppress the voice that was screaming out for help. I had to let myself in rather than turn away from what I felt. You need to realise that there comes a time when you need to push, yet the memories will pull you back. They latch on to what you had to recreate the past. All we ever do is hide. We close our eyes and count to ten, so we wouldn't be reminded of what we had back then. The truth is, we don't move on by forgetting. We move on with acceptance. You accept what once was and move towards what is. You're stuck inside a cycle of wanting to be whole, so you disallow yourself to keep control. We love a thousand times over, yet never completely love ourselves. Soulmates may exist, but the one true soul you have to understand is yours. Nothing else matters except for how you treat yourself.

Every memory contains a fragment of who you used to be, and when formed together, they build upon your history. I knew every thought included someone I neglected, and sadly, it was me. I want you to remember everything that hurts you. I want you to think. I want you to overthink, because this is exactly how you let go of heartbreak. I've experienced it. I've felt it. I want you to be like me. Promise me you'll do this. I want to save you from the self-created madness, because sometimes, we need to be reminded of how to be real. People like us always seem to fall, and it's hard, you know? We keep believing we'll get better, but the losses add to what we know. I'm sorry, but I need you to overcome rather than throw away what you've become.

Close your eyes and smile over memories you shared. I want you to be glad that you experienced the purest kind of joy with whoever seems to haunt you, but I want you to realise it could have been with anyone. You see, we look for connection because we want to combine our worlds together, just so we can feel like we belong. The person you want to forget is somewhere else, but these memories can be replaced with others, and that's what we fail to realise. We're so fixated on finding a perfect match, when in reality, no one can be perfect. We're human. We're flawed. We're made to break, as sad as it may be. I initially thought I missed everyone I lost, but I figured out I miss the idea of having someone there. I was scared of standing here alone. We all are. We want to fight the world together, but when we're left stranded, we feel like a lone survivor.

There's nothing you can do to make things right again, and the more you live inside the past, your future seems to struggle. I've always been the type of person to never give advice, because influencing decisions is something I would never want to do. Now here I am, telling you to let go of everything you feel. I want you to take that part of you and accept it for what it is. You're stronger than your mind is telling you. You see everything that's happened? It's nothing. It doesn't define you as a person. I want you to realise that life and pain come hand in hand, and you should be glad to have lived through an experience, even if it added to your grief. We live. We breathe. We think. It's the way the world keeps moving, and It's how I found myself catching up with all its twists and turns.

I'm an overthinker, and the more I overthought, I thought I would forget her. It was never going to happen, and I knew it deep inside. We're not made to forget. We're made to over-feel and overthink, but how do we get over what we labelled as forever? The simplicity of moving on is one which I had to teach myself in stages, because growing is about making needed changes. No one can ever fix you, because once you're broken, you adapt to all the issues. That's why every part of you will hurt as you move across your timeline. The worst part of being human is that we fail to realise what we're given. We barely live at all when we're in trouble. We dream about the future, but our vision is clouded by a past we wish we could have changed.

The truth is, love never really broke me, because I was broken before I ever felt connection. I was trying to belong in a world that felt like it was closing, and I never fit into the puzzle I was chasing. I was lost inside my mind, expecting to get better without trying. You know that empty feeling? The one that makes you wonder why you're here and what you're doing? I felt it every single day, and I couldn't find escape. I couldn't move on from the ache, and now I know why every instance of this pain was too much for me to take. I kept believing in this dream of somehow getting better, and tried to push aside these memories to bring back the faded colours. I was wrong to believe it would help me in the slightest, because I fell deeper into silence.

We have this strong desire of wanting to be close to others, because we feel as though they can save us from misfortune. I was afraid to say goodbye to people I held closely, but I saw the truth in its entirety. We all have two choices—to stay still or to move forward. Most of us will be stuck trying to find a way to keep our relationships alive, but the ending is always one which we're surprised of. Every connection has a timer, yet we try to outstay our welcome, and we end up disconnecting. This is why we can't come to terms with loss, because we never expect our worlds to crash and burn, and when they do, we only ever hurt. The most important person in your life is you, and believe me when I say this, your sanity is something you must cherish. You can't keep repeating the

Papikins

same mistakes that you've lived through, and it may be hard to do, but it's the only way to save yourself from falling.

I want you to realise what I do. You read every single word as I string them all together, and as you can see, they're linked to different parts of me. I go from one thought to the other, desperately trying to understand the direction which I'm heading. I think about the past and the present, but never look towards the future. I used to be afraid of looking back, but it's part of history. It's my story. I look back to understand. I look back to give myself motivation to keep on moving. I realised it's the only way to let go, because forgetting will only suppress the feelings that you have. I'm an open book. I don't keep secrets because I know that they'll destroy me. I want people to connect to these raw emotions without me feeling guilty. I want to be real and honest, and honestly, honesty is the strongest part of my personality. I found the key to moving on is acceptance, and now I realise that every chapter of my story has a beginning and an ending. I now know to turn the page rather than try to burn the book.

Papikins

Will we have tomorrow?

I feel the world crashing and burning, and it never seems to stop. I have this constant need to be loved, but I'm losing hope to be remembered. I wonder about the future and what it could mean. I'm always asking myself the same old question; will we have tomorrow? I'm scared of waking up one day and not being able to breathe. I feel like I'm still adventuring into life and all its mysteries, but what if the journey stops? Will I be happy, or will I feel lost? It's a thought that's loudly on repeat. The future is uncertain, but here I am still hopeful. I want to see tomorrow. I want to feel today. I want to save myself from yesterday, because the past is all I know. Life has changed, and I'm further from where I was before. I don't know what to do, and I don't know where to go. We take everything for granted, not expecting the unexpected. We never see things coming until it's just too late. The days feel colder now, as the winter takes control of what we hold, but do I even hold anything at all? I feel helpless and defeated, yet I still think that I can overcome it.

Papikins

Unreturned

You're ashamed of what we had, because you knew it wouldn't last. You filled me with regret as you cut into the thread that was holding us together. I knew that everything would end, as our story seemed to falter at each and every turn. I gave everything I had to make you feel like you were mine, but somehow, the feelings weren't returned. You were the better part of loneliness when nothing else made sense. I attached myself to us to make it hurt a little less. I wish I could have been what you desired, but now I've lost a friend.

Papikins

Lost you

I know it pained you to see me lose my smile. You wanted more for us, but I could never be enough. I was trying my best to love you with these thoughts inside my mind, but the way everything fell apart makes it seem like life is supposed to be unkind. I was aiming to be better, and now look at where I am. I see a lonely person staring back at me inside the mirror. You were the greatest part of my existence, and when I lost you, I felt my world was crumbling.

Goodbye

The nights were all we ever had. I remember the taste of your lips and the sadness you hid behind your eyes. You were perfect. You were strong. You were everything I couldn't be, and still, your face is haunting me. I would have died so many times just to see you smile, but then I wouldn't get to hold you through the coldest nights. You were my hope among the stars, but you never got to see me shine. You would be proud of who I am, and if you wouldn't, it truly doesn't matter. I came to the realisation that I'd rather move than stay here seated. That's the problem with affection. We'd rather turn back time than view the memories as nothing more than history. This is goodbye to love. This is goodbye to us.

Empty space

Death is a painful reminder that we're human. It happens all of a sudden, and we feel the empty space that's left behind within an instant. We relive the moments because the future is uncertain. We're thrown towards the skies but hell is where our minds begin to wander. The peace we took for granted had slowly been dismantled. We try to take a sip of water, but it hits us just like venom. We fear the worst will happen, and when it does, our lives are torn apart. There's no escaping death, but we have the choice to push through every day as we progress. We forget that time exists. We coast around and let it pass. There's no reason to. We make the world our own, as we find out who we are when we're inevitably left alone. It's hard to comprehend, but the truth is, life is meant to be lived, even if it hurts.

Close my eyes

I miss you. I miss the stories we used to tell, and the laughter that we shared. I miss how infectious your happiness could be. There are words I wish to tell you, but you're nowhere close to where I stand. You're somewhere out in heaven, and I hope to see your face again. I've been holding on to pictures, yet they only make me crumble. It's been getting harder to breathe when I'm reminded that I have nothing left but me. There's a certain kind of sadness that seems to push me to the edge. I think, and I think, and I think too fucking much to even feel as if I'm fine. The skies somehow turn to grey, as I sometimes lose myself in space. I've tried to write you back into the scene, but sadly, it's only just a dream. I'm still here without you, and the days keep getting colder. I wish I knew why the world was made to be so cruel. I know I have to move, and I know you'd want me to. That's the sad reality of life and death. We love and we lose, but we're never out of strength. We build back everything we lost, and we gain a thousand times more than what we had.

It's death that seems to ruin me. The death of time, and the death of those whom I admired. I wish I could go back to when our time had started, but it's life. We never get the chance to relive what we had. I would do anything to touch your skin, or get the power of your scent. I miss your smile the most. Your laughter was infectious, and I wish you could see all the beauty I've created. You would be proud of the person I've become. Well, I hope so at least.

105

Lovedemic

I know that time has passed, but I still tend to look back at the past. I remind myself I'm here because of you, and it's all I seem to need to float around the blue. We were inseparable at times, and I miss the days where we sat in silence and let each other cry. It may have been upsetting, but it was the most human side of life. I sometimes write you letters, but I keep them locked away from prying eyes. It's therapeutic to be reminded of what I've lost. I wouldn't be able to be strong if it weren't for you. You made me realise I shouldn't be afraid to remember who I was. It's a part of history. It's the reason why I breathe. Every moment has been mine, and if I forget about humanity, I know I wouldn't shine.

There comes a time where we have to keep pushing through with life. It's hard. It truly is. We have to say goodbye to what was and live within what is. The memories we shared will forever be a part of who I am, and I thank you for your time and energy. I'll try my best to live for the both of us, or for the many that I've lost. It's life. It's death. It's the reason why I need to catch my breath. I have to realise my story is unwritten, and even without your presence, I'll try my best to shine. I know we live to die, but I'm glad to have spent my time with you, and I sincerely hope we'll meet again whenever it's time to close my eyes for good.

Papikins

Xi

I search for all the answers, but all I seem to do is feed the darkness.

Papikins

Darkness

I want you to know the truth. I want you to realise what I do. These words may be poetic, but I've always found them to be pathetic. The only reason why we feel connected is purely because the rhythm feels electric. You're beautiful, and it's hard to even say it, because I barely even know you, but the way you've come this far with me, I somehow think I do. You make me believe in love again, as if soulmates still exist in a time like this. Maybe we belong together in some way, not romantically, but mentally. We found each other in the universe, even if our time together hurts. I promise I can also be your happiness, but with all these promises, I may become a liar. I'm afraid of how you see me when I can barely see myself. I don't want to disappoint you, but eventually I will.

You feel so familiar. I wish I could remember the past life we may have lived, but maybe those are stories, and this is the only place we've been. I'm glad I can share this moment with a stranger far from where I'm standing, or sitting, or even laying down. I have no idea where I'll be, but you, you're somehow here with me. It's the beauty of writing, isn't it? We form worlds behind our words, but they cut deeper when we're exposed. I hope you understand that moments just like ours are what fuel the fire in my heart. The flames are all I seem to know, yet they've turned to ice out here in the cold. I never thought I'd be this far into the blue, but as my heart began to bleed, the sadness took over all the good. I write, and I write, but after all is said and done, the words are merely letters in my eyes. I foreshadow what is told until brilliance is made and my voice echoes through the page. I leave you wanting more. I make you crave it, don't I? I effortlessly tell our story, as if we lived together for some time, but as I paint these pictures in your head, you fall into my trap and we connect. I'm an artist, a poet, and a God. I create worlds beyond what others could describe, as I pen a story out in ink to give you reasons to find peace.

We connect so easily, but only if the timing is correct. You and I were meant to be, but why does it to have be so painful? I never wanted to hurt anyone, but sometimes, I step away from kindness and let reality control me. We're designed to run from the unknown, and when we feel too much, we hide our heads among music, movies, and books. We visualise the differences between fiction and reality, as we try to shield our instability. It's escapism, isn't it? We lose ourselves in words to find escape from an empty world. We never truly realise we create the narrative. We stand still when we should move, and we walk away when we should stay. It's how some stories never form a perfect ending. We fear for the worst to happen, and suddenly, we fall apart without a reason. The truth is, there's a reason for everything.

I barely noticed how alone we truly are. We may feel it from time to time, but we never understand that loneliness can save us. We never take the time to appreciate emotions unless they're associated to raising pleasure. We form bonds which never should have been, and we fall in love with the undeserving. It's always about connection. We're aimlessly on a road to find out who we are, but all we do is attach our hope to those around us. We wish to be imperfect together, and that's what drives us unwillingly. We're incapable of finding strength within ourselves, because the narrative has always overshadowed how we feel. We're told to find love and start a family, and how we should strive to connect to strangers to stop ourselves from feeling lonely. There is no happiness. I've stated it time and time again. Want to know the secret? There is no loneliness either. Everything is a state of mind, and when we think too much, I swear to God, it feels like we're wasting life. I remember when I was too afraid to think, but then I realised I'm in control of who I am inside.

We sometimes forget about our souls, and it may be hurtful to overcome our tragedies, but the mind is sacred and the soul is made to be imperfect. We make mistakes and wonder why we're hurting. It's humanity. It's what we are and how we dream. The darkness had always been a friend of mine. It greeted me when I didn't feel alive, but what does that truly mean? I was here, but I was vacant. I was breathing, but I fell silent. I wanted to find myself inside destruction. I knew the world was mine, but I never felt the need to take it. We can either lay our heads to rest or try to hold the universe. We build our boundaries to stay seated, but if we never learn to fly, will we ever reach for greatness? I've led a life of honesty, or that's how it feels to me. Maybe I'm a liar, but it's hard for me to see. It's self-perception, isn't it? We view ourselves as less, but believe we know the best. It's why I rarely understood myself. I made decisions based on impulse yet most of them felt forced. I was out of control and I couldn't see my worth. It's a tragic story of regret, and it hurt like hell whenever I wanted to connect.

I would always try to trust when I had nothing left to give. It's the only way I thought I could find love. I wanted someone to wipe away my tears, even if my stories went unsung. It's the dream of being human that prevented me from living. We wish for something real, but when reality is far from where we're standing, we're disengaged from all the light around us. We step into the dark, wondering who the fuck we are. I've tried to grab the stars, but they were never there for me to reach. It was always in my head. I wanted to be free, but I kept my heart locked inside a cage. I'm in love with the idea of connecting in the darkness. I've lost my smile a thousand times, trying to pretend I had a chance at love, but when my love was gone, I was further from the sun. I was committed to staying quiet, but little did I know, the silence would push me further into darkness. We avoid the dark for so long, but never realise it's a part of who we are. Every year of fighting the urge to keep it all inside is another year we never should have wasted.

The truth is, we neglect ourselves entirely. We try to save the world, but what good would it be if we barely save ourselves? I've lived to tell a thousand tales, but in the end, I've only lost myself. It never occurred to me that I was chasing happiness. I would stare at my reflection and wonder who I am to others. I was afraid of being seen differently to how I see myself. I could lie to you so easily, but I won't. I could barely look into my eyes. I didn't want to know why

I felt the way I do. The depth and clarity were blurred. I just wanted someone to notice. I wanted to feel less alone in this fucked up world. It's the darkness, isn't it? We hide among the shadows until our minds are hollow, but it's impossible. There's never a time where we stay thoughtless. We devalue emptiness because it drives us to feeling hopeless. It's those empty moments that give us power. Sadly, many of us tend to shy away from reaching deeper. We're afraid of what we'll find lurking in the distance, even if all we find is silence.

I wanted peace. I wanted the screaming to stop for only just a second to see if I'd somehow be complete. I should have been more curious, because what I found was me. I was lost inside the dark. It was never my intention to drift far into the void, but the only thing I hid from was the person I never could become. We build to become better, and the darkness is where we hide our insecurities. It's the only honest part of us, and if we attempt to disconnect our depth, we'll never learn to move beyond the hurt. It's life. It affects us. We dream to stay away, but when those dreams are gone, we're afraid to be awake. I've always had an addiction to breathing, but my breath was the reason why I felt detached. I inhaled an experience which filled me up with doubt, but that was my problem. I never exhaled to drown the demons out. I never had the chance to grow apart from what I knew. I used to believe the darkness was my undoing, but the more I sat in silence, it was further from the truth.

I was lost in dreams for so long, but never realised they were merged into my current state of mind. I'm glad I get to share a moment with a stranger. I'm glad I'm not alone. We're never truly as alone as we believe. We wonder who we are, as we search for answers to where we are in life. It's the reason why you're here. It's the reason why I write. We just want to feel alive. We rarely get to breathe when we're flooded with disaster. It's the thoughts that throw us down into the fire, but if we never burn, we'll never have tomorrow. The darkness is what I feared, but after everything I went through, I realised I couldn't face the truth. I tried to find myself in other people, and I stood in all the vacant spaces, but none were reserved solely just for me. It's how I pushed away from what I felt. I disrupted change because I lacked the will to greet the darkness when it was begging to be seen.

We're unable to let go. We hold on to dark clouds and sleepless nights, as we resist the urge to cry. The tears I've shed are a reminder of what I've lost and what I've found. It's a manic state of consciousness which alleviates my sorrow. I've had a lifetime full of dreams yet none conveyed tomorrow. I was dreaming while awake, yet I could never see the future, only remnants of stories that I've told. There's beauty in simplicity, and throughout my agony, I've seen a sense of symmetry. We wait for time to pass to forget about the past, not realising there's no option to go back. It's as if we allow ourselves to falter, as we step into obscurity. I grew to hate what I've become, but the truth is, I never knew who the fuck I was. It's never too late to realise where you're standing. There's no reason to hide away the dark if all you're fighting is the person that you are, and believe me, you're enough to heal your scars.

113

Incomplete

I want you to be real with me. I want you to be honest, and honestly, I deserve a bit of honesty. I want you to tell me what's wrong with me. I want to know exactly where we stood. I want you to help me understand, because to be completely truthful, I still fight the loneliness of love and the bitterness of losing us. I always thought I'd find the missing piece towards my puzzle, but here I am still incomplete and fragile.

Omicron

Breathe.. I'm begging you to breathe. If you never catch your breath, you'll only lead yourself to death.

Papikins

Pi

Closure and clarity are a threat to sanity.

Papikins

Sinner

I've never been strong enough to stand alone. I've never been well enough to keep myself afloat. I keep pushing to be real, but there's secrets I conceal. I don't know who to trust when every friend I've had has disappeared somewhere in the past. I've been searching for myself, but I've never known exactly who I am. I've changed throughout the years, and every time I get close enough to understand, I'm back to where I started. It's a numbing way to live, because I've been hiding from the only constant in my life. It's as if I'm destined to walk alone with lies. I've had trouble with pretending to be a happy person, but now I seem to smile even when I'm breaking. I'm tired of being seen as less than perfect when I know I'll never reach it. I'm a saint and I'm a sinner, but when I make mistakes, I'm labelled as a monster. The truth behind most of my decisions are tied to who I think I am, but I've never seen myself to even give a damn.

I moved a thousand mountains yet still amounted to almost nothing. It's the loss of self, isn't it? We take our inner needs for granted, and the id and ego become disjointed. We're primitive in nature, but the strings hold us firmly pieced together. I suppressed the urge to be a sinner, but sometimes you have to see the world entirely to be able to get a glimpse of what you fear. I was afraid of my reflection. I was afraid of being human. I knew I had to keep my secrets, but through all the hidden truths, I couldn't find a deeper

117

meaning. We resist to live in our entirety. It's a harsh truth to a sad reality. It's the reason why we're scared of honesty. We fear to be rejected if we expose ourselves completely. I would always search for fragments of myself in other people, but I only saw the devil. It made me want to burn away tomorrow, but I've never been that type of evil. I may be a sinner through and through, but I'm purely made of chaotic good.

My eyes are always closed. It's as if I'm oblivious to what I do. I hurt the ones around me, even if I never mean to. I cloud my judgement with indecision, as I try to make sense of why I feel so distant. I create problems with my thinking. It's always the thoughts that seem to hurt me. They overpower how I feel, and suddenly, I have to find the strength to leave. It's how I lose in love and friendship. I'm tired of trusting too hard with a fragile heart. I can't even find myself when I'm begging to feel alive. I'm scared of being close to anyone, because I know they'll try to see beyond my tired eyes. The only part of me that ever feels alone is the one I never got to know. It's buried deep inside my broken soul. I just wish it didn't show, but it slips between the cracks when I attach myself to hope.

I'm always on this search for happiness, even if I say I don't believe in it. I'm a hypocrite, or maybe I'm just human. There are many sides to me which go against what I believe. I keep falling but I never reach the end. It's an endless loop to a usual trend. I'm used to being thrown against the wind, but I'm tired of repeating all my sins. There's no escape from what I've done, and as I push aside the emptiness, I wonder what kind of monster I've become. It takes a lot of courage to not hate myself at times. I blame myself the most whenever I find myself alone. I wonder why I couldn't be enough, and why my weakness was never being strong. I've always been incapable of carrying myself the way I want. I think about the person that I am, but it's far away from truth. There's always been a hidden layer, but I don't intend to lurk within the shadows any longer. I need to accept myself for what I am. I'm just another sinner.

My only sin has been neglecting who I am. I always thought it was a problem with the world. I repeatedly fell into mistakes, yet never learned from every ache. We rarely understand why we feel so helpless. It's as if every faded dream is a reminder of why we dwell in sadness. The truth is, I've never been the same. I thought I had a constant state of mind, but that was just another lie. We try to reach for heaven when we're closer towards hell. We avoid the agony of knowing ourselves entirely. We'd rather stay in the same position than rebuild with new decisions. It distracts us from the sins that we've committed until our tragedies are too far gone to be accepted. I'm not going to lie to you. Not today. Not tomorrow. Not ever. There are days where you'll feel nothing. You may have lost yourself in that moment, but it'll keep repeating. We adjust to what we're given until we realise we're back to where we started. The most beautiful part about life is that it only stops when we're left standing. We're never truly lost if we keep moving. We just have to find the person we're becoming.

Rho

We fall into each other's arms only for a moment, and when the moments gone, our paths lead us to another.

Papikins

Sigma

We accept lies as if they're currency, and we tender them to the best of our ability.

Papikins

Tau

What is it to dream if nothing is ever certain? What is certainty when none of us desire to be human? We see the world as if it's drawn on to a canvas, yet the artist never had the chance to finish what they started.

Papikins

Faded

I'm tired of reliving moments we never should have had. I'm tired of pretending we were perfect when I knew we should have ended. We sometimes sit in silence, as we wonder what we had and why we lost it. We want to know exactly when our love had faded, but we never have the chance to recreate the story. The truth is, we view one side and neglect the bitter truth in its entirety.

Silence

I want to trust you, but I can't. We've been through hell and back, and we'll never be the same again. It was never my intention to try to let you go, but you forced my hand with the lies you never should have told. I wanted to grow old with you. I wanted the sun to rise a thousand times over while I held you in my arms, but the thoughts of us are gone. The only part that still remains is the past and who we were. I used to believe that I found happiness, but after all the pain you put me through, there's nothing left but silence.

124

Upsilon

I only wanted a perfect soul so others could finally see my worth,
yet little did I know that my heart would turn to stone.

Papikins

Phi

I feed off recognition. I comb my fingers through my history to feel every hurtful memory. I give. I take. I throw it all away. I want to be connected yet no one seems to stay. I'm the loneliness behind a sickness that somehow grabs me by the lungs. I wish it could be different, but I'm still made to be imperfect.

Papikins

Chi

What is my truth? I'm alive yet limited. I crave to be an addict, but only for oxygen and poetry. I want to breathe life into my tragedies, but I'm torn between decisions of where I am and who I want to be. I make mistakes that only hurt others who get close to me. I'm rapidly mutating at a rate that no one else can see. I'm scared of how I feel. I need to let it out, but I know the changes will ruin what I've built. I need to find my peace. I need to find release.

Psi

I keep my heart inside a cage. I'm an alien as some would clearly state. I refuse to be a label in the eyes of a species where Cain could kill his brother Abel. We believe in sin, and we hurt without warning. We're unkind to ourselves due to a lifetime of evil. We bleed to feel alive, yet we're hopeful to survive. Reality is flawed and humanity is fucked, but in time, we can change the narrative and say enough is enough, but until then, only doom will come.

Papikins

Omega

I am the cruellest part of my existence. I am the stars that shine without assistance. I am the voice inside my head that screams without resistance. I am the child who could have been but never was. I am the one who gives for nothing in return. I am the blood, sweat, and tears of a life that I once lived. I am kind and I am hateful. I abide but stay a little sinful. I am infinitely amazing, and truth be told, I am majestic, poetic, and a thousand times effective. I am an essence of mother nature, and I am the one who paves my future. I am the Omega.

Papikins

Stranger

I've been staring at the clock, wondering where my time has gone. I remember when I was young, but now I'm just a stranger to the kid inside the mirror. I wanted to find myself somewhere in the blue, but now the days are getting shorter, and I feel further from the truth. I'm afraid to walk towards the future, but honestly, I'm stuck inside of past endeavours. I've been fighting off the urge to feel as though I'm worthless, but what have I done to be deserving? I make mistakes when I feel as if I'm certain, and it only leaves a wound when I'm sure of what I'm doing. I'm just tired of trying to be a perfect person. I'm tired of having good intentions but somehow being labelled as the villain. I just want to make things right, even if I have no jurisdiction.

Papikins

Romance is alive

I've always been hopeless, and when I fall in love, I'm helplessly addicted. It's strange how emotions keep on changing. Romance is dead would echo through my head, but when I saw your face, blood rushed into my veins. The dull beating of my heart turned into a melody again, and I swear to God I found solace in your smile, as I only saw an angel standing before my eyes. I've been dreaming for a while, but every time I'm next to you, your skin brushing against mine somehow brings me back to life. You're talented and beautiful, but every thought I've had has never led me to how I feel right now. It's miraculous to be connected to another soul. I would always fight the loneliness of standing here as one, because the universe took away my will to love. I'm drawn to everything you do, from the devious smirk across your face to the way you hide your pain. I dream about you every night, and the world is so much brighter in my mind. We're in each other's arms, and I feel so fucking young. It's as if every chapter that I've told had only fell apart to bring me to this moment, and I hope what we have is close to perfect.

There have been times where I've given up entirely, but I never lost hope in finding someone who'd inspire me. It's what I've always wanted, and through my love of poetry, I built the perfect sonnet. I want you to know what love is, and I want you to somehow feel it. We're attracted to energy more than anything, and when we cross paths inside the current, we feel a spark between a

Papikins

stranger and the soul that we've been hiding. I never knew how hard it is to find myself again. I never thought about it. It never crossed my mind that I was lost. The minutes turn to hours as we overthink the world around us. I never took the time to think about my life, and the reasons why I needed someone there to be my rock. We sometimes need support, yet we're too afraid to ask for help. We've been shattered into pieces, and we have little trust to give. It's love. It's always been love. It pushes us towards our darkest depths just to find the missing piece to give us hope. We're incomplete at different stages of our lives, and before I met you, I thought love was just a hoax.

It's hard to trust when you've been treated less than what you're worth. You find excuses to keep a wall around you so others have less room to find out who you are. You become too closed to even care about, even though you're dying to feel real. It's indulgence, isn't it? We feed into our urges to prevent ourselves from hurting. We don't want to feel the way we did before, because it only ends in heartbreak. I know how it feels to be alone. I've wanted to shut away emotions, but it only ever seemed to hurt me. I was defending my peace with little thought to what I needed, and what I truly needed was someone to shield me from myself. Sometimes all we need is someone else. We need them to fight away the demons, because some of us are incapable of being on our own. It's the harsh truth to come to terms with, but if you truly didn't think it, you weren't as hopeless as I intended. It's how I feel right now. I'm in love with the thought of someone else, and it feels as beautiful as I remember. I'm in love with the thought of you, even if you were once a stranger.

Loving too much has always been my problem. I had nothing left after everything that happened. I wanted to hide my head and wait until the sun would set, but when I finally got to hold you, I didn't want the day to end. You were my ticket to salvation, and it may sound unrealistic, but you pushed me to be decisive. It's all we hope for when we're falling. We want to hold our posture and find our ground again. You leave me breathless like I've somehow been infected. It's as if the world has stopped, and it's only ever us. I kept fighting off the urge to stay here by myself, but when you're standing here beside me, I'm closer to the world. You make me worry less when I'm reminded that we share a certain kind of sadness. It's all I've ever needed. I've always had a fear of loneliness, but when we're laying there together, we're lonely with each other. It's the dream, isn't it? We wish to be alone with someone else. Someone who understands us. Someone who makes our lives feel more welcome, because when we're stuck without them, we have nothing left other than reflections.

I'm sometimes afraid of loving you, because I know that one day everything will fall apart, and our time together will be another dent inside the past. I saw forever in your eyes, but still, it's hard to keep romantic dreams alive. You're the only one who knows my hidden side. I love to show you the reality that lurks behind my smile. I can finally be myself whenever I'm around you. I can tell you every story without shedding tears and feeling lonely. I sometimes wonder why someone so angelic would be close to someone foolish. You make me want to love myself, and that's all I ever needed. I had to know that I was worth it, because through every tragedy, I lost the greatest parts of me. It's reassurance, isn't it? I need to be reminded of the person that I can't seem to see, but when I'm with you, I somehow feel like me. You have me wrapped around your finger, and I feel like I'm in danger. You're the brightest days ahead, and I'm glad none were ever wasted. I would do anything to make you smile, and if by chance we had the time, I would wash away your worry, because it's also a part of mine.

I have a fear of being left behind. It's the reason why I'm scared to take my chances. It's how we are after losing strength within our hearts. We're afraid to disconnect. We want love to find us, but we're scared that romance is gone forever. We watch everything burn before our eyes, and when the winter comes, we're thrown into the cold without any sense of warmth. It's what happens when the fire starts to die. We feel incapable of love, but the truth is, we do it to ourselves. Everyone is worthy of love, even the quiet ones with clipped wings not strong enough to fly. I always thought romance was dead, but it only dies with us. No one else can remove it from who we are, even the ones we used to love. Romance is alive and well, even if one day, our lovers are only stories that we learn to tell.

Papikins

Etched into my heart

There was love and there was hate, but what I felt for you went beyond what I could take. I wanted to free you from the sadness, but I only made it worse. I added on to pain when I thought I could have saved. I was fighting for our love, but the problems still remained. I was in a losing battle, and I kept giving reasons for you to run away. I was always there for you, even if you didn't want me to be present. I would sit and stare into your eyes, wondering why they make me feel alive. I loved your touch above all else. It warmed my mind whenever your hand would slide right into mine. I had always been afraid of walking back towards depression, but when I stood beside you, my mind was less imprisoned. You became my sole addiction, and that may have ruined us entirely when we both had different visions. I wanted to be your saviour. I wanted to make you smile, and honestly, I like to feel as though I did, even if only for some time. It's love, isn't it? I was endlessly in love with a thought inside my head. I attached myself to nothing and became a slave to every word you said. I could blame you for what happened, but I'd rather understand why I disrespected myself by staying.

I remember how it used to be, but now we're merely another memory. I could have sworn we were going somewhere, but in the end, we wore out all our options. There's only so many times you can try to fix what's damaged until you realise the warmth has vanished. We were unable to fill the void, but we stayed and kept it quiet. I was trying to be yours, not knowing you were never mine. I lacked the courage to be alone, so I clutched on to what we had. I thought I could bring it back, but what's dead never lives again. I wanted romance to be exactly what we shared. I wanted to slip into your gaze, and find what makes you tick. What is love without teasing? What is love without belonging? I saw myself beside you, but I still couldn't tell where we were going. I turned a blind eye to keep our love alive, but was there any love at all? It seems to plague my mind. The one I loved before is now a stranger in my eyes. We built each other up just to let each other go. We turned the page on every chapter, but the ink was running dry. I tried to write more lines, but in the end, I had to say goodbye.

We have a loneliness inside us, and like I've said a thousand times before, it never seems to sleep. It pulls us in when we feel as though we're weak. It knows exactly when to show its face. It grabs us tight and holds us still, until we start to weep. I've fought loneliness forever, but when things fall apart, so does my state of mind. I've been afraid of letting go. I've been afraid of moving on. I want everything to stay as is, because I'm scared to be alone. I thought you'd understand me. I thought you'd stay, but people never do. They leave as quickly as they came. I believed in us. I had faith in our future plans. We were meant to start a family, but our time together overran. We moved beyond the credits and there was nothing left but black. The darkness was all I ever saw when I felt our love had died. I couldn't comprehend the outcome of what happened to our lives. I wanted to make you stay, but nothing could bring us back when all we had were lies.

I could have kept pretending, but I honestly hate to be a liar. I didn't want to belittle what I felt, and all I seemed to feel was loneliness and guilt. There were days where I disconnected from the world. I would look at my surroundings and see all these happy faces. Why was it so hard for me to have that? I sat alone outside, wondering who I am, and if I'll ever truly smile. I needed someone there. I needed to feel complete, but I couldn't. I was sick of seeing red wherever I would go. I was sick of seeing couples when I lost my chance at love. The truth is, I was desperate to feel enough. I've lost my worth more than I can count. Did I really ever have it? I would stay when I should leave. I would fix when I should break. There were many issues that made me question whether I fit between the spaces. I lost my self-respect, just to give everything I had to someone who never truly wanted me. I relied on you to be there the way I was for you, but I guess the silence spoke a thousand words. You tore my happiness apart, and now you're another scar that's etched into my heart.

Papikins

Home

I want to forget. I want to forget about you, and about us. I want time to wash away the memories I held against my heart. I need to let you go, but this part of me that loves disallows me to disconnect from what we were. We were beautiful. We were an untold story never made to have an end, but there was an ending, wasn't there? It was as bitter as can be, yet I tried to keep pulling at our strings to keep you here with me. I wanted you to stay. I wanted you to love me. I wanted you to save me. I couldn't see that time had pushed us to our death. We were hanging on to what I call the edge. You were my everything, but that's another lie I tell myself to stop feeling like I'm lonely.

You see, there are times when I remember who I was. I think about your smile and how you brightened up my life. It's always you, isn't it? It's never about me. It's never about how I overcame my emptiness and found the will to love. It's never about the times I shut out all the noise and made it through the coldest nights. I remember you so vividly, but the truth is, I was part of what we had. I was the joy among our tears and the calming of our fears. I could never see myself as clearly until I let you go. I was riddled with self-doubt. I felt worthless and as if my hands were bound. I finally see that I forgot to love myself. You may have been my home, but after all these years, I realised it wouldn't have been built if I didn't learn to be alone.

138

Papikins

Poison

I had these endless thoughts of you. You were running through my head at a speed I couldn't comprehend. I fell in love with the blurred image of your face, because I was lost in our embrace. You infected me. You injected poison into my veins and gave me hope that I'd be saved. I needed you in sickness and in health, but we never got to take the oath. I was in love with this dream of us for so long. I wanted reality and fantasy to somehow merge together, but life never goes to plan. The truth is, I was lost within a trance. I attached myself to nothing, as I avoided finding out who I truly am. It was never my intention to lose a friend, but as the story goes, we only used each other until the bitter end.

In her eyes

I would stare into her eyes and notice all the truths that she would hide. They were bright yet she was blind. She would look away from danger just to feel a sense of purpose. She wanted to believe in happiness, but fell towards the dirt as she clawed her way back into existence. She fought with demons in her head, but all they ever did was take advantage of all the words she never said. She was alone and she was broken, but to others, she was warm and so outspoken. She hid beneath a wicked smile, but it was drawn against her face, as she thought her presence was pretence. She was scared to show herself to anyone, be it family or friends. They admired her beyond what she could see, and she was vying to be perfect just to please. She kept her distance when she needed space to breathe, and when she gasped for air, she barely found relief. She kept thinking, and she kept thinking until her smile was torn to pieces. It was life. It was loss. It was the lingering thoughts of what it means to be enough.

She was lost inside her thoughts, and the addiction to find perfection grew as the minutes turned to hours. She cared too much for friends who'd only fade. They left a hole inside her heart, and gave nothing in return, as she begged for them to stay. She would wonder if she's worthless, or if she'd ever find her place. There were days where her world would crumble. She was scared of letting go, so she'd lock the hurt inside her head and replace it with emptiness

140

instead. She forged a perfect smile, but it never truly meant that happiness existed. It's always the smile, isn't it? She desperately wanted to be somebody else. She wanted to touch the clouds and feel their warmth against her skin, but all she ever felt were tears running down her lips. The bitter taste of desire was too much for her to take. She wanted to find peace, but her memories were buried deep, and she had nowhere left to store the tragedies of being. She could have had it all, but she could never look beyond betrayal.

She was searching for survival. She never thought she could conquer the world in its entirety, but sometimes people fall. She never had the chance to redeem herself. She never had a choice to be the person she envisioned. She was imperfect. She could never reach the top, and it was everything she hated. She would claw away at skin, trying to find release among the universe, but all she ever did was cause pain and disbelief. She felt alienated from the world, but it never seemed to show. She wanted to hold her ground. She wanted the weary look upon her face to be more than just a frown, so she lied and she lied until she forced herself to smile. Like I said, it's always the smile that hits the hardest. We rarely wonder if it's authentic or if it's staged. She wanted someone to notice, but even if they did, she knew that they would leave. It was a familiar story in her life, and one which she locked away inside.

The hurt of abandonment is one which we never have a hold of. She walked ahead in loneliness. It was all she ever knew, as her heart raced towards an answer. She had a thousand questions, but only needed one to give her what she desired. She wanted to understand the reason why no one stood beside her. She lost a hundred faces who only turned to names. They were once what held her glued together. They were destruction and support. She thought forever had been set in stone, but as they disappeared, her strength would leave her body. She would feel a little guilty, as she found it hard to let them go. She blamed herself the most. She pushed and she pulled. She had to erase the bad and the good. The thoughts of loneliness and the curse of being left behind plagued her mind at night. She was a reflection of who she used to be. There were times where she would cry, but her tears were detached from the reasons why. It was sudden. It was as if the skies had turned to grey and her mind followed the world as it decayed.

There were moments in her life that made little sense at all. She would wonder why she felt alone, and why the colours had dimmed before her eyes. She never saw the world as vibrant. The days were vacant and the nights were stagnant. She found herself alone but could never label anywhere as home. She had to release her anger on anything that resembled pen and paper. She held the brush many times before, but the silence was overbearing. Her mind was flurried with regret, and as she stood beside the canvas, she never knew exactly how to fill it. She painted pictures in her mind, yet the ones that came to life were never easy to convey. They taunted her with past mistakes. They sunk into her skin as she drew them out in ink. She was creatively gifted, but her thoughts were the reason why she never had the courage to chase her dreams.

Papikins

Lovedemic

She barely had control. She sat in silence with her favourite song playing on repeat, and as the music faded, she'd skip back to the starting beat. She felt discomfort when it was quiet. There had to be noise to calm her senses. She wanted to feel more human rather than lead her mind to ruin. She was an overthinker. She wanted her thoughts to merge together, but they only led her to disaster. Her days would slide to darkness, and the nights became more restless. She would toss and turn before she slept, wondering why she felt a disconnect. It's life, isn't it? We take everything for granted until we lose our smiles. We long for happiness to save us, but will it ever come? Will the moments turn to hope? Will we dream about tomorrow as much as we did the day before? I want to be honest with you, and I think you deserve some honesty, because honestly, I'm sorry. There are times we find ourselves roaming towards distractions. We never seem to understand that emptiness forever drives us. It's the empty feeling that there's something missing. That's the missing piece. That's the part of us that somehow leads us to despair. I know you feel it. I know you stare into the mirror and wonder why you don't feel perfect. I do it without realising. It hurts. I know. Believe me, I know. I've always wanted to be let in, and enjoy a moment with a stranger. Maybe I'm alone.

The problem is, we attempt to find happiness in places where we feel restricted. We assume what we have is what we need, and what we want is what escapes us. It's sad, isn't it? I view the world as temporary, but where do I go after? Where do any of us truly go? We search for hope but are only led towards a nightmare. I thought,

Papikins

and I thought until the truth was never found. The reason why we feel alone is because we think too much, and it's a fucking problem. We try to connect the pieces of who we are to what's around us. We want to be complete. We want to find a purpose. We've been drowning for so long but never swim towards the surface, and believe me, it's always there, but it's hard to find it. It's how life twists and turns. We aim for the skies but are shot down before we get to fly. We want perfection. We want to be connected, but all we ever do is slip between the spaces.

There's nothing more tragic than being addicted to connection. It isn't purely about connecting with another, but to the atmosphere we fail to breathe in. We want to extend our value, but end up wanting more. We're selfish, we're greedy, and a little bit far gone. The truth is, I wanted everything to fade. I had this thought inside my head that I could finally be free, but freedom is more than wanting to escape. I died a thousand times inside my head, and it only pushed me to the edge. There's a cold sensation running down my spine as I write these words tonight. Maybe you're somewhere out there. Maybe we were destined to share each other's burdens. I know you find it hard to understand what it means to love your imperfections, but what I see is a broken shade of beautiful. You may not see yourself as worthy, but worth is built on the lies we tell each other. We never fit within the universe, or maybe we do. We create a world for two, just like I have here with you.

I sometimes get lost in how I feel. I find it hard to function when I can't tell if my thoughts are real. I used to close my eyes and count to ten, waiting for the truth to be revealed. I never knew how destructive I could be. I was searching for perfection. I was hoping to find happiness. But I truly had no reason. You see, life is meant to be lived rather than thought about. We can chase our dreams forever, but forever will one day end. I was tired of standing still. I was tired of staring at the pictures of what was and reliving what I should have left behind. I kept drowning in these memories, but the harshest truth is that I never should have stayed somewhere which could have damaged me. We prolong the pain. We let it linger until reality is gone and we're fictitious.

She never believed that she could find herself. It was part of her design. It was the reason why she kept her jaded smile. There were moments where she was quiet. She could barely speak a word because she felt like no one cared. She had to push herself to breathe when surrounded by her peers. I could never tell why she felt so distant, or why her heart was full of discontent. I wanted to remove her mask to see what lurks beneath. I needed to look closer. I truly wanted to see her for who she is, and what I saw inside her eyes will forever haunt me, because she's a mirror image of humanity. She's purity and tragedy without a sense of honesty. The truth is, she's both you and I behind the sadness in our eyes.

About the author

Hopefully we meet again, but for now, from my heart to yours, this is goodbye.

Cyrus Ahmadnia

Instagram – @papikins

Twitter – @papikinz

Website – www.papikins.com